Midnight Renegade

HAYDEN LOCKE

Midnight Renegade
Cover Designer: Silver at Bitter Sage Designs
Editor: Rachel Mitchell
Formatting: Hayden Locke

To all the girls who struggle with imposter syndrome.

I dare you to believe in yourself.

You are magic.

AUTHOR NOTE - ALL THE THINGS

Thank you so much for taking a chance on Midnight Renegade! Here's a few things you might want to know before reading.

TROPES

One-night stand, instalove, baseball romance small cliffhanger (don't come for me it's a prequel novella)

TAGS

MF, one-night stand, New York City, New Years Eve, golden-retriever, let me take care of you, toys as teammates, new year new me

CONTENT WARNING

This novella contains mention of a parental death and the fall out after. This novella contains detailed sex scenes that include elements of dirty talk, choking and toy use.

NEW YEAR...
NEW FEELS...
NEW CHANCES.
SAME DREAM...
GET DICKED DOWN BY A DIRTY TALKING BASEBALL
PLAYER AS THE BALL DROPS.

Welcome to your baseball era.

CHAPTER ONE
Willow

The ceiling of his bedroom comes into focus on my phone screen. I recognize the shell shapes from all the times I was on my back unfulfilled in the orgasm department—seven lines on each shell with fourteen shells per tile.

Multiples of seven are supposed to be lucky. Apparently not for me.

My eyes water and I blink back the tears. I can't cry. Not now. I gave him three years of my life but you'd never know that based on the sounds of him fucking his assistant and moaning her name.

I struggle to breathe, each slap of flesh that echoes from my phone speakers a stab to my heart.

I'm accustomed to things not going my way. From the moment I was born, I didn't fit the mold set for me and have been forced to make concessions ever since. Daughter of the York estate, there wasn't room for mistakes in the eyes of my mother, and my father wasn't around between fighting criminal cases and making sure he was out of court to make it to the stadium before the first pitch was tossed. Which left me as my mother's doll.

I didn't mind it when I was young. In my eyes, my mother hung the moon and my father the stars. I worked hard to be everything they wanted and more, but when my curves grew too full or my aspirations too high my mother was all too quick to remind me what a failure I was.

So you see, I'm used to being both the letdown and the one let down, but this hits different. He was supposed to be my person. My support. Tonight was supposed to be our night. For fucks sake, I thought he was going to propose.

I'm an idiot.

I suck in a strangled breath, the weight of my insecurities heavy on my chest as I blink back the tears that threaten to fall.

"She's not you, Gigi," Patrick pants and I can picture him cupping her neck as he thrusts. His signature move. "You're beautiful. She's a dead fish on a mattress. When I marry her it will be so I can build us the life you deserve."

The life she deserves?

The. Life. She. Deserves.

My shock gives way to anger, and despite my broken heart I finally find my voice.

"Fuck you, Patrick," I yell at the phone.

Why couldn't he have hit end instead of accidentally swiping to connect?

But then you wouldn't know, a tiny voice in my mind echoes and I instantly hate it.

Ignorance would've been bliss for just this one night. He knows how much this fundraiser means to me. Why couldn't he have just shown up for me this once? He knows I have limited support tonight. My best friend's, Leighton, water broke. My other best friend, Indie, was with her at the hospital. That left me—someone who is terrified of public speaking—to make the keynote speech. And while my father is also here tonight, he's more of a *live life like it's his oyster* and doesn't understand the low-key panic that tends to sneak up on me like a rogue wave.

I just needed someone there to reassure me I'm not going to fuck this up and fail the kids counting on me.

Patrick knew all this and chose to play sick and ghost me for fake orgasms and a kiss from his mistress at midnight. And he had the audacity to wonder why it's so hard for me to trust people.

A small gasp brings me back to the present. I glance up and see Mrs. Benson clutching her pearls and glaring daggers in my direction.

Shit.

Of course, she picks the moment I'm discovering my boyfriend with his pants down to walk out of the ladies' room.

As the wife of a senator who isn't particularly fond of my father, and by extension me, it surprises me they bothered to show up to the fundraiser at all. She's also the biggest gossip I know. I can see the headlines now: "York Heiress Has Meltdown at her Inaugural New Year's Charity Event."

They'll leave out the part where I caught my boyfriend of three years cheating on me, if they ask for a comment at all. Either that or they'll blame it on me for being too ambitious.

I roll my eyes at the thought. Call me crazy, but I don't aspire to be a trophy housewife. I want to make a difference in the community. I want to be remembered for more than my name and my trust fund.

My father is the only one who understands that. It's what bonds us.

That and the love of baseball I inherited from him.

"Willow?"

Damn it.

I smile politely at Mrs. Benson and turn and walk down the hall, away from her prying ears. Looking down at my phone, I find a very naked Patrick with Gigi clutching his sheets behind him.

"Why are you calling me?" he barked–hackles up like he isn't the one having the affair. "Aren't you supposed to be at the fundraiser?"

"I am," I snap. "Where are you?"

Patrick blinks only just putting together I can see Gigi behind him.

"Fuck," he breathes. "It's...it's not what it looks like."

"What does it look like then? You know what? Nevermind. I'm sure you have a perfectly valid excuse, but I can't do this right now, Patrick," I tell him, eyes narrowing as I try my best to seem unphased.

He knows my looks though, and he reads me like a book. I'm trying to give *don't push me* vibes but my heart is breaking, and my anger hasn't taken hold so it comes out as more of a *how could you* vibe.

My phone beeps signaling the battery is about to die.

"Please Willow, baby, let me explain."

I shake my head, a single tear falling against my will. He was supposed to be my happily ever after. We weren't the perfect couple, but we were a powerhouse—the lawyer and the socialite. We were...

No.

Panic grips my spine.

We were my mother and father.

My stomach lurches and I do my best to force air into my lungs.

How had I not seen it?

I'd done everything I could to avoid this. And yet there's a tiny voice in

4

the back of my head telling me it was all for naught. I still managed to end up with a lawyer. The only difference is I'm not the one who cheated. He did, just like my mother. The difference is my father took her back, over and over.

I won't make the same mistake.

"Willow?" The worry in Patrick's voice is palpable, like he senses his golden ticket being shredded to pieces.

"We're done, Patrick. I'll send your shit to your apartment."

"Come on, Wills, we can work this out. She's nothing. You know the long nights."

Gigi scoffs in the background, but I don't hear what she says next when I say, "Goodbye, Pat." And hang up the phone.

The walls feel like they are closing in, and I've got nowhere to run to. There are too many people counting on me. But I can't stay there. Not where my tears can be used against me.

The glint of the New York skyline, decked in its New Year's finest, catches my eye through the giant windows at the end of the hall. They lead to a terrace with a nine-story drop and no escape, but my mind only sees freedom.

I race to the door and force myself into the frigid December night, breathing in the city I love, grateful for the anonymity she provides. Out here I'm not Patrick's girlfriend or the CEO of Renegade Hearts. Out here I'm just Willow. A woman who's a little heartbroken and a lot lost.

The wind whips my blonde hair back and forth as I tip my head skyward. I let my tears fall freely and I whisper a prayer that the new year will be kinder to me.

This is my year.

It has to be.

I just have to make it to midnight.

CHAPTER TWO
Bishop

I can't believe I'm considering this. Nothing good will come of me going out with the rookie, and yet it's better than the alternative.

Reaching up, I drag my fingers through my hair, pushing back the ends that touch my ears. I really should have gotten it cut before tonight. Even if Norah insisted it was fine. I believe the exact word she used was dashing, but if I had to choose, I'd much rather go for more of a fuckable look. Of course, I couldn't tell her that. She might be one of my best friends, but she's also married to my other best friend and teammate Jackson Roberts, who wouldn't take kindly to me stealing his girl.

Norah meant well. As the president of the Get Bishop Laid club, she was only trying to boost my ego. Even if we both know I won't be taking any of these women home tonight.

Been there. Done that. Lost a lot of money in the process.

My eyes drift across the ballroom decorated in a roaring twenties theme with gold deco added to every surface. I take in every detail in an effort to avoid the stares of my teammates waiting patiently for my response.

I just wanted to play baseball. I never imagined all this bullshit would come along with it. Unfortunately, as a leader and one of the faces of the New York Renegades, there is no way our PR team was about to let me skip out on the good press that accompanies this event. Who wouldn't want to spend New Year's Eve dressed up at a party with endless champagne and views of downtown New York that make even the hardest of hearts swoon? At least that's how it was pitched to us when we were *volun-told* we'd be here since the founder of the foundation is the daughter of Richard York, our team's owner.

"Come on, Law, it's going to be a blast. Just picture it." Tommy Woods, the rookie Jackson and I took under our wing last season, leans into my shoulder and gestures his hand in front of us as if he's laying out his master plan. "We're gonna leave this stuffy party and trade it in for the VIP experience. Women dancing on boxes in tiny spandex, while other women high on new year, new me vibes, line up to grind against us and indulge in their daddy issues for a night of no-strings-attached fun."

I plaster a fake smile on my face and shove him off me, before tipping back my glass and finishing the remainder of my whiskey.

Nothing about that sounds like fun to me. It never has. Even at his age when I was first called up to the big show and had more money than I knew what to do with, and arguably less fucks to give, I still didn't want it. I wanted to play baseball and have the kind of love my parents did. Now I'm a thirty-three year-old, almost divorcee, being told I should be embracing my hoe phase after the loss of my marriage.

I'm not convinced.

Do I want to get laid? Yes. But in our line of work, women only want us for our status as professional athletes, and I've already learned the hard way I'm not made for that kind of relationship.

Not that I knew that when I met Corrine. She played the part perfectly—checked all my boxes. Smart, funny, down to earth, didn't mind the occasional fivefinger necklace when I was balls deep in her. She told me she wanted a family, and I was her one true love. And I believed every word. Her only downside was she wanted me all to herself and didn't like my friends. It was a glaring issue and everyone saw it but me. To me, it was cute she wanted all my attention.

Until she didn't.

She isolated me from everyone and then, when I was out of town playing ball, she was banging Joe, the architect to the stars, followed by Cameron, the son of an oil baron. At least the architect was only a one-night fling. During our season, Ritchie Rich had all but moved into the Central Park apartment Corrine just had to have, and everyone suspected it but me. I wasn't clued in until I walked in after losing the pennant and found him fucking my wife on the kitchen island.

Heartbroken, I moved into Jackson's guest bedroom. A week later, I filed for divorce. His family—Norah and their seven-year-old daughter, Phoebe—welcomed me with open arms.

A month and a half later and I should be more upset than I am, but I think deep down I saw the writing on the wall a year into our two-year marriage. I just didn't want to believe it. Excuse the hell out of me for daring to believe everyone wants an epic love to share their life with.

Newsflash—they don't.

The problem is my heart tends to forget that. Which is why I'm hesitant to go out with the rookie tonight. It's the first time I'll be putting myself out there since filing for divorce. Even though I know what I want, the last thing I need to do is allow myself to get attached to another gold digger looking for the spotlight.

Then again, a night out with Tommy can save me from listening to Jackson and Norah's epic New year's sex. They may think they're quiet, but if that were true, why do I know as much as I do about the kinks they swear they don't have?

Do I care? No.

Am I jealous? Absolutely.

"Are you sure you can even keep up with the rookie, Law?" Norah jokes, giving me a pointed look from across the high top table where she stands beside her husband. Wearing a pink gown, she looks every bit the princess he treats her as. "You've got at least ten years on him, and debatably, more gray than brown in that scruff you think is sexy."

"It is sexy," I counter, lifting my chin and stroking the even beard I know she secretly likes.

Tommy scoffs. "Are you ever going to stop referring to me as the rookie? There are new guys on the team. I'm a vet now."

"Absolutely not," I say at the same time Jackson says, "No." We turn toward one another and tip our heads back, laughing. He lifts his hand to his forehead and taps his temple as if to say *great minds*.

Tommy lets out an exaggerated moan, and a few attendees standing at the tables around us turn and glare in our direction. One lady is dressed head to toe in crystals, with a permanent scowl. She scoffs and mutters, "Who the hell are they?"

The mother fucking NYC Renegades, I almost answer, but I'm pretty sure that won't garner us the good press the team hopes for. We might have done better than the other team across the river, but we're still the bastard team of New York no one likes to admit they root for.

Resting Bitch Face glares in our direction and turns her nose up before heading to the bar for what I'm sure is a martini. Shaken not stirred because that's how Bond drinks it.

I roll my eyes and chuckle to myself.

I hate these fucking events. No matter how many of them I attend, they've never grown on me. I'm a southern boy, raised in a place where fancy was a school dance in the auditorium with spiked punch. This is a far cry from that. These people don't care about the children or the camp they're building for them. They just want a reason to socialize with other people like them. People who have far too many zeros in their bank accounts. They live for nights in a ballroom lavished with more sparkles than the Times Square Ball. And maybe if they're lucky, they'll be the ones to donate enough to have their name commemorated on the new dining hall. Corrine loved coming to these events and rubbing shoulders with the upper class, which only further proves my point.

Assholes, every single one of them.

"I don't think the locals like us very much," Tommy whispers playfully.

"Speak for yourself. They love me," Jackson says, pretending to pick a piece of lint off his jacket. "It's just you, Rookie. They can taste the uncultured swine that permeates from your pores."

"Laugh it up, Roberts. You won't be so jubilant when I've got an heiress on my arm."

"Oooh, seventeen-point word for the Rookie." I give a soft punch to his bicep.

Jackson slings his arm around Norah and leans in, pressing a kiss to her temple. "I'll take my forensic psychologist over your future heiress any day."

Something deep in my chest seizes and I have to work to ignore the resentment that blooms in its place. I hate it's there at all. They are my best friends, and I have no business feeling this way, but fuck, I want what they have.

"Ugh." Tommy sighs. "Why do you two have to be so damn sweet? Do you know you're doing it or is it something that just oozes from your pores when you get married?"

"You get used to it," I say at the same time Jackson shrugs and Norah laughs. I almost add that it's not a married thing. It's a soul mate thing because Corrine was never like that.

I wince. Again with the red flags that I never noticed.

"You'll find your aisle seat someday, Rookie," Norah offers.

"My what?"

Fuck, not this again.

"On that note, I am going to refill my drink before dinner and toasts." I've heard Norah's theory about finding someone who wants the window to your aisle seat—or vice versa— and how it's the superior relationship compatibility test more times than I can count.

Funny story, Corrine didn't pass that test, either.

I scan the table, noticing my friend's empty glasses. "Anyone else need a refill?"

Tommy lifts his glass. "Another for me."

"Me too," Norah chimes in.

I meet Jackson's gaze and raise a brow in question.

"I'm good. One of us needs to stay sober enough to get us home."

Norah scoffs and leans away from her husband playfully. "I'm a fantastic drunk."

"Who likes to wander into random pizza shops and proclaim pineapple is the holy grail of pizza consumption."

Shaking my head, I walk away as they debate the finer points of toppings, thankful for the opportunity to delay having to decline going out with the Rookie.

For the record, pineapple should not go on pizza, but I know I'll never convince Norah of that.

The ballroom is set up in a giant U-shape with a stage front and center, a dance floor below it, and tables with elaborate centerpieces surrounding it. Everything sparkles, and I'll be lucky if I can walk away without glitter permanently embedded in my borrowed tux. I head to the back of the room and make my way to the bar on the left side which has fewer people waiting for drinks.

Two bartenders hustle behind the bar, and I'm lucky when the older of the two recognizes me and instantly heads over.

"You're Bishop Lawson."

I grin. "Last time I checked."

"Holy shit, I mean sorry." He stumbles over his words and a sheepish smile stretches across his face. "I mean, it's an honor to meet you."

I return the smile with one of my own and assure him. "The honor is all mine."

He chews his lip and I know what's coming next. It's the same with everyone who sees us "out in the wild". Some of the guys hate it, but I don't mind. This is part of the job, and in all honesty, if I can make someone's day then who am I to snuff out that bit of joy?

"I know this is totally inappropriate, but my kid is a huge fan of yours. Would you mind taking a quick selfie?"

"Of course, man."

He pulls his phone from his pocket and spins around, snaps a quick selfie, and then takes my drink order. When he walks away, he's smiling wider than before.

I grab the nearest napkin and a pen and scrawl a note to his son.

"You are going to make that boy's year," a deep voice says beside me.

Looking up, it's the owner of the Renegades, Richard York, beside me with his signature megawatt smile. He's tall, not quite as tall as me, but the way he commands attention, you'd think he was a giant. Unlike the majority of people in this room, Mr. York's presence is almost comforting. It's easy to see he genuinely cares about his players and their families, taking the role of the grandfather everyone wishes they had.

"It's the least I could do," I say as I finish signing my name. "Fans like him and his son are why I get to do what I love most."

He nods his approval and gives his order to the younger bartender.

As the bartender begins making his drink, the lights around the ballroom dim, and the master of ceremonies—some comedian I've never heard of— announces dinner and toasts are about to begin and encourages us to find our seats.

"That's my cue," Richard says, grabbing his drink and placing a hundred-dollar bill on the bar. "Will you do me a favor and pop out onto the balcony and let my daughter know she's up next?"

I open my mouth to argue that I need to take drinks back to my friends, but he grabs a server and asks him to take them for me.

"Thank you, Bishop." He wraps his hand around my bicep and gives it a gentle squeeze, paired with a soft smile. "I would go myself, but she's not exactly thrilled with me at the moment and I don't want to upset her before her speech. I may have tampered with the seating arrangement just a little and ruffled some donors' feathers."

I don't get out a single word before he turns and walks away, leaving me and my whiskey to go deal with his daughter, who sounds like an absolute delight.

I manage to find the hallway with a wall full of windows leading to the balcony. In the middle, pacing like a madwoman in emerald, is Mr. York's daughter.

I might hate her on principle, but anyone with eyes can see she's gorgeous. She's got painted red lips and stunning blonde waves, but what surprises me is her curves. Most of the women inside are nothing but skin and bones because that's what society tells them to be, but not Miss York. She's got hips that beg for fingers to grip them and, from what I can see through the slit that reaches her waist, thighs that would make excellent earmuffs. My gaze travels down her sinful figure to her feet. My brows skyrocket. Are those black Chuck Taylors?

She turns on her heel to pace back in my direction, and I get a good look at her face.

Ah, shit.

She wipes at her face, but even in the dim lighting, I can see the tears streaking her face.

Fuck my life.

I didn't sign up for this.

Richard can find his own daughter and drag her back to the event she's supposed to be hosting.

I turn around, fully prepared to ignore this little side mission, when guilt hits me square in the chest, followed by my conscience berating me. *If it were any of your sisters, wouldn't you want someone to make sure they were okay?*

I hate my answer.

Damn, my bleeding heart.

CHAPTER THREE
Willow

I didn't think this through.

People crowd in Times Square below—singing, dancing, and waiting to ring in the new year in one of the greatest cities in the world. They have no idea I'm locked out on a balcony—fifty floors up—freezing my ass off in a ball gown, trying not to give into the elephant sitting on my chest.

It's my fault, really. When panic sets in, all rational thought goes out the window. Of course, I didn't think to check the door to make sure it didn't lock from the inside.

Fucking Patrick.

It isn't his fault I'm locked out of my own event, but I need someone to blame. Something to cling to so I don't focus on the fact my teeth are chattering and my lips are likely blue under the bold red lacquer Leigh insisted I wear. Chances are I'll be hypothermic by the time someone finds me.

At least I had the smarts to wear my Chuck Taylors instead of strappy heels. Comfort before beauty.

I rub my hands over my arms to distract myself, which is why I don't hear the latch of the door.

"What the hell are you doing out here without a coat?"

I whip around, and my gaze connects with the owner of the gruff voice rushing toward me.

"Wait!" I cry and dart toward the door. "Don't let the—" Click. My heart sinks. "Door close."

He spins around and reaches for the door, jiggling the handle, but it's useless. I tried. Along with frantically banging on the door in the hopes someone would hear. If my phone wasn't dead, I would have called for help. I don't know whose genius idea it was to pick a hotel where there's a hallway between the ballroom and the terrace.

Oh, that's right. It was me. I didn't want the ambient noise of New Year's in New York to ruin the gala, but I wanted the option for donors to watch the ball drop at midnight.

The glittering ball with giant numbers taunts me from across Times Square. I don't even like New Year's in New York. It's crowded and messy and everyone seems to forget to celebrate in favor of getting the perfect selfie of their New Year's kiss.

My would-be savior turns around, and I get my first glance at exactly who joined me in this freezing hell.

I swallow hard. It's Bishop Lawson, star catcher of the New York Renegades. Even if I wasn't the owner's daughter, I'd recognize Bishop's chiseled jaw, dusted with salt and pepper scruff, under insanely prominent cheekbones any woman would kill for. The Renegades might be considered the *other* team that plays over the river in Queens, but when you're arguably one of the best catchers in the league, and going through a high-profile divorce, everyone knows your face.

"How the hell did you get locked out here?" Bishop asks, and I can't help but wonder if he's all brawn and no brains. A shame, really.

I roll my eyes. "The same way you just did."

His lips press together, a sign he's unimpressed with my sass. His eyes scour the balcony. I'm sure for a way out. Once he's satisfied I'm not jerking his chain and we're actually locked out here, he closes his eyes, brings the tumbler in his hand to his lips, and downs the rest of his whiskey.

I imagine the burn feels great down his throat, settling in his belly. A liquid sweater is better than the nothing I'm working with.

As if he read my mind, he sets his glass down and shrugs his tux jacket off before stepping forward and draping it around my shoulders.

"Thank you," I murmur.

He tips his head forward. "What I meant is, what the hell are you doing out here in the first place? It's fucking frigid."

Despite his chivalrous gesture, annoyance laces his voice, but I'm too busy noticing the way his biceps threaten to pop the seams of his dress shirt to care.

What is wrong with me? I just found out my boyfriend has been cheating on me for God knows how long, and here I am ogling the first guy I come across. Then again, my sense of logic has been known to check out when fight or flight kicks in. So, I might as well welcome the distraction. It's better than focusing on Patrick, speeches, or hypothermia.

Or it was. Now I've just added them back into the circulation of problems to solve.

Bishop steps forward and wraps his hand around my forearm. "Ms. York?"

"Hmm?" I manage to answer, but my mind has already moved on from the snackable man in front of me.

"Again, why are you out here?"

"It's Willow, and you asked how before, not why." I step to the side and look at the floor to ceiling windows and the door he just walked through, checking for the hundredth time to see that no one else has wandered into the hallway.

Of course, my luck isn't that great, and apparently, neither is Bishop's because it's empty.

When my gaze returns to him, his brow is furrowed and his head tilted to the side, like he's unsure what to make of me.

Me too, Bishop. Me too.

"Do you have your phone?"

He shakes his head. "I left it on the table, thinking I'd be right back."

Of course. The universe has decided tonight is the night nothing can go right.

"Are you okay?" he asks.

Not even a little.

"Um. Yeah." I sigh, but it feels like I've reached my breaking point. "I just needed some space. You see it's been a bit of a night. Usually, my best friend, our CFO, gives the speeches because I'm terrified of public speaking, but she's in labor and our other best friend, who is an actress and arguably a much better option, is with her. So, that leaves me to give the speech in front of a ballroom full of judgemental asshats whose money our foundation really needs. Then when I needed a bit of support so I didn't back out and run, I called my boyfriend and got the joy of listening to him tell his secretary how much of a dead fish I am in bed and how she's ten times prettier before he shoved his dick in her repeatedly."

Bishop's brow raises at the same time his eyes go wide.

"Shit. I'm sorry I shouldn't have laid all that on you." I huff a laugh and begin to pace again, even though internally I'm cursing my nerves for turning me into a blubbering fool.

This guy probably thinks I'm crazy.

I shake my head and twirl the end of one of my curls around my fingers. One foot in front of the other, I focus on my breathing.

In.

Out.

Repeat.

This is why I called Patrick. I needed him to talk me down. I can't go in there and give a speech in front of all those people. I'm going to humiliate the entire foundation and ruin our chances of getting the donations by blurting out something embarrassing like how I hate these stupid events, and they should be willing to give money out of the kindness of their hearts, not some stupid auction for things they don't even need. Or how Patrick is a complete fool if he thinks I'm a dead fish. He's the one who only likes missionary with the lights off. To think I had a night planned for him with a bag full of toys and even wore sexy lingerie just for him.

"I don't know. Learning you have a bag full of toys might open up a few wallets."

"Shit." I freeze mid-pace and curse under my breath. "I said all that out loud, didn't I?"

I look up, and he's wearing a devilish smirk that no doubt has dropped panties everywhere.

"Absolutely."

I press my hand over my eyes and spin toward the balcony railing, all the while wishing for a hole to open up and swallow me whole. *Just take me as I am.* Maybe if I die, people will feel bad and donate, anyway.

With nowhere to escape, I inhale a shaky breath and turn back around. Bishop's got a hand over his mouth, and his shoulders are shaking slightly. He's laughing at me. Not with me. At me.

Someone kill me now.

"Come here," he commands with his arms outstretched and a soft smile.

Instantly I'm skeptical. Who just asks someone to leap into their arms? Especially someone who has just unloaded an epic ton of embarrassing information and is pacing like a lunatic.

"Willow, you're freezing and if it were my sister trapped out here, I'd want someone to take care of her. At least until help arrived."

Against my better judgment, I embrace my inner Indie and take a step forward into his arms. She's going to have a field day when I tell her of the moments spent against Bishop Lawson's chest.

"Plus, if I had to guess you're on the verge of a panic attack and the pressure will help."

"I hadn't noticed," I say, huffing an easy laugh and resisting the urge to snuggle into his chest. He's right. The pressure does help. There's also the fact he's the perfect height. Just tall enough that his chin rests on the top of my head. Which is saying something considering I'm five foot nine. And his smell—cedar and bergamot—is fresh yet also somehow has a hint of musk that lingers. It's all man. Nothing like Patrick or any other man I've been with.

He wraps his arms around me, and we stand there tangled together in relative silence, save for the ambient noise of New York that serves as a constant. It's almost as comforting as Bishop is.

"Are you feeling better?"

I nod, despite the fact I'm full of shit and shivering against him. Tipping my head back, I peer up at his face. At that exact moment, his tongue darts out and wets his lower lip, and my gaze zeros in on the action like a moth to a flame. His lips are nice, full, and pink despite being outside in the cold.

Maybe it's the lights or maybe it's the magic of New Year's or the fact I just got cheated on, but despite it being a terrible idea, I want to know what his lips would feel like against mine.

Damn. I really am a hot mess.

His eyes snap down to my lips and back up again, and for a split second, I wonder if he's thinking the same thing. Then he blinks, and the moment is gone.

The silence that stretches between us verges on sour and awkward, so I quickly change the subject. "How did you know? The panic attack, I mean?"

"Aside from the pacing? My sister gets them. I figured out pretty young how to help her through them."

What I would have given to have someone who cared. Pesky tears line my eyes, and I'm thankful he can't see them when I whisper, "She's lucky to have you."

"I like to think so." Bishop chuckles and begins to rub his hands in small circles on my back. "Still scared about the speech?"

Shrugging, I lie, "A little. Public speaking isn't really my thing. As I said, usually our CFO gives the speeches."

"I think she gets a free pass for popping out a kid."

An easy laugh escapes me and a sliver of air hits my neck, eliciting a shiver. "I suppose I won't hold it against her."

He shifts to accommodate me, wrapping his coat high and tight around me. It's an innocent gesture but only serves to press us closer together, accentuating every bit of thick muscle he possesses.

Including the one between his legs.

It's not fully hard, but it's absolutely there and I can't unknow that little tidbit of information. Or how above average it feels.

A little squeak spills from my throat, and I clench my thighs together in an attempt to stop the pulse between them.

Bishop goes still. His chest rises and falls with a slow breath, and I manage to adjust my hips so my pubic bone no longer presses against him at the same time he clears his throat.

"Uh…tell me about Renegade Hearts. Why did you start it?"

My jaw clenches tight. Not because I don't want to answer him, but because there's a small part of me that wishes I was confident enough to explore the fact he's just as turned on as I am.

Who am I kidding? It's just a natural reaction to being so close to one another. He could have any girl he wants. I'm sure a curvy socialite with a penchant for panic attacks isn't at the top of his list.

I force a smile that's more for me than him and start my rehearsed answer. "Mostly I started it because I hated being a corporate lawyer. I wanted to follow in my dad's footsteps, but it turns out I don't have what it takes to be cut-throat like that. I tried a few different things, but I kept coming back to braids."

"Braids?" he asks with a hint of confusion, and I can picture his brows raised like before. "Braid? Like hair?"

"Yup. Exactly like that. You should have seen the first time my father tried to braid my hair after my mother died. It was a disaster. I was brushing out knots for hours. It was a growing pain I never considered when I lost my mom."

Bishop tenses and for a beat there's nothing but the sound of his thundering heart against my ear. He gives me a gentle squeeze and whispers reverently, "I can't even imagine."

"That's why I started the foundation. Losing my mom was hard on me. There were moments that a girl could only share with her mother, and I no longer had one. But it was just as hard on my dad. I wanted to create a place where spouses and children could adapt to their new normal without feeling like the world is crashing down on them."

"I never would have considered the little things like that."

"Are you close with your parents?"

"Very. Well, as much as you can be with eleven brothers and sisters."

"Yikes. Now that I can't imagine."

Bishop chuckles, and the sound is a welcome warmth to our shitty situation. It's light and addictive, and I can't help but wonder what a full laugh from him would feel like.

"It's hectic and there's never a dull moment, but it's also incredible. I always had someone to play catch with or help with homework."

I can picture him as a little kid, a mop of dark hair. Running around with his siblings, perpetually covered in dirt, playing baseball, and protecting them from the world.

The image sparks a flame of longing in my chest. What I would have given for that kind of childhood.

I press my head against his chest and a war breaks out between my heart and logic. I'm not sure if it's the cold, his proximity, or maybe it's just my frayed nerves and the fact I'm mentally exhausted, but I don't have the energy to put up a front. So instead, I let him in.

"I wanted that as a kid. But my dad shipped me off to boarding school after my mom died. Not because my dad didn't want me around, he just didn't know how to be a parent to a preteen daughter. I didn't mind most of the time. It's where I met my best friends, but it wasn't the same as being surrounded by family. I lived for the summers when I got to spend time at the ballpark with my dad. It was the first time I felt like I had what everyone else did."

"What do you mean?"

Oh, just that despite the fact my mother was the center of my world, I now realize she was an absolute witch who lived and died by the ideals of high society, and I'm lucky to have escaped without an eating disorder and an arranged marriage.

That's what I want to say, but I don't, because that wouldn't be proper. Even from beyond the grave my mother's standards are ingrained—never risk the York Legacy.

I inhale a steading breath and give a weak smile. "Family. Before my mother died, I didn't know what it was like to truly have people I could count on. I was raised by nannies and expected to be seen and not heard. It sucks losing a parent, but I got my dad back after she was gone."

Bishop tenses against me. When I pull back just enough to see his face, his eyes are locked on mine, filled with what looks like a mix of pity and compassion.

I huff a laugh in an attempt to break the tension. "I…you weren't expecting that, were you?"

He doesn't answer right away. Instead, he just stares at me like I'm a puzzle with pieces that don't quite fit.

It's uncomfortable. Especially since, had I just kept my mouth shut, we wouldn't be here.

With an internal grimace, I move to step away, but Bishop's arms tighten, stopping me.

"It's okay—" I start to say, but he cuts me off.

"No, it's not. I…" He chews his lip as if he's trying to choose his words carefully. "I really thought when I walked out here I was going to find an entitled bitch throwing a fit because her father messed with her seating chart."

"How do you know I'm not?" I say with a raised brow. Anything to steer us into lighter territory.

"For starters, you're wearing Converse with a ballgown and I'm pretty sure those earrings are in the shape of the emblem of the rebel alliance. Anyone who sides with the rebels couldn't possibly be entitled."

I reach up and finger the studs.

"Can I tell you a secret?" He nods and I lean in and whisper, "I've never seen the movies. A little boy at the rec center gave them to me because he said I reminded him of Princess Leia."

Bishop tips his head back, a guttural laugh bursting before muttering something about blasphemy under his breath.

Holy hell.

I was right. Bishop's laugh is magic and leaves my whole body tingling. It's joyful and infectious, and I can't help but smile right along with him. I have no idea why this man who thought so little of me when he came out here is being so kind. Especially after everything I've said and done, but I can't deny it's exactly what I needed.

A large gust of wind knocks into us, and I lose my footing against Bishop. He adjusts his stance to steady us, tightening his hold. The wind continues, whipping my hair around my face, before I tuck it into the crook of his neck.

His scent was heady before, but being tucked against his skin makes it downright intoxicating. I inhale a sharp breath, committing it to memory.

No man has any business smelling so good.

Bishop shudders and lets out a string of curses.

Shit.

I just can't help but embarrass myself in front of this man. What was I thinking? I barely know him and I just sniffed his neck like he's a damn flower.

I catch my lip between my teeth to stifle my groan of embarrassment and keep my eyes glued on Bishop's chest, not wanting to look up and see him laughing at me.

At the very least, he's going to have a great story to tell his teammates about the time he got stuck on a balcony with the owner's daughter. Though I'll never be able to show my face at the stadium again.

Bishop tucks a finger under my chin and lifts until my eyes meet his.

There's kindness and just below that, a soft heat that warms my insides. It's just unnerving enough that I don't know if I should stay or run.

He fingers a stray curl and tucks it behind my ear, keeping his palm pressed to my jaw after he does. "You know, if you tell donors the story you just told me, I guarantee you'll meet your goal. It's genuine and heartfelt. People love that."

I shake my head, trying not only to make sense of his words but also the way his hand feels against my skin. "It's better if I stick with the script. At least then I know my nerves won't reveal anything too embarrassing."

He shrugs. "Suit yourself, but I think there is something endearing about embarrassing. It's real. And if you want, I've got some tips on how to manage the stage fright."

"You do?"

"Sure. You forget I'm in front of the press after most games. The trick is two-fold. First, you've got to believe you're a badass."

I cock a brow and a shallow laugh bursts out of me. "That simple, huh?"

He nods and keeps going. "Absolutely. Say it, I'm a badass in a ballgown."

"I don't think that's going to work."

"You have to believe it. And if you don't, know that I do, so you're already halfway there."

I roll my eyes. "Okay, so after I affirm myself, then what?"

"Then, when you're up there, you pick one thing to focus on. One thing that isn't going to waiver. It could be the lapel pin on a reporter or the clock on the back wall. Really, anything you can latch onto. Then you talk to that thing like it's the only thing in the room. It's like when you stand on one foot and they tell you to focus on something stationary so that you don't fall over. Find your one thing in the room and everything else melts away."

"And you say this is founded with research?"

"It's always worked for me. My sister, too. She's a dancer."

"Well, if it's a Lawson family secret, I guess I'll give it a try."

"You're going to do great, Willow. Give them a glimpse of the woman I just met and you'll have your camp funded by the end of the night."

It's a compelling thought. One I'd never entertain except maybe in this twilight zone moment wrapped up in the arms of Bishop Lawson. But that's just it. Just because he believes in me, doesn't mean the rest of the donors will. This twilight zone wasn't meant to last. The night always comes to extinguish the light.

"I—"

The door to the terrace swings open, halting me from giving him a lesson in playing the game and all the reasons I can't be as honest with them as I have with him.

Our bubble bursts when we both turn and see Candy, my event

coordinator, standing there.

I abruptly take a step back, though I know I'm not fooling the observant redhead.

"There you are, Miss York!" she exclaims. "We've been looking for you everywhere. Dinner is almost done and you've got to get ready to get on stage."

Unlike Bishop, she stands in the doorway as she speaks, preventing the door from locking.

Pink fills my cheeks. "Sorry, we got locked out. I'll be right there."

"Okay." She nods, examining the schedule on her clipboard. "Just don't be too long. We've got to stay on schedule for the ball drop."

"Of course."

Candy drops the door stopper and her eyes dart between Bishop and me before she heads back inside.

I let out the breath I'd been holding and turn to Bishop. "Thank you so much for...everything."

He chews his lip, something he does a lot, and nods but doesn't say anything else. I don't know what I expect him to say. Something. Anything. He doesn't, so I give him a soft smile and head for the door.

Two steps are all I take when Bishop's hand shoots out, wrapping around my wrist. He spins me toward him until I'm once again pinned against his chest. Except this time, there's nothing innocent about it.

His fingers tangle in my hair. He tips my head back, and I barely have a moment to inhale before he crashes his lips to mine.

Bishop Lawson is kissing me.

The city melts away, and my heart pounds against my ribcage as he works his lips against mine. His tongue demands entrance, and I can't stop the moan that slips from my lips. Which he swallows as if it's his last meal.

Gone is the soft-worded man who claimed my warmth and sanity as his personal mission. He's replaced by the one kissing me like he intends to own me. He's raw and manic, like Jekyll when he gives way to Hyde.

And I'm living for it.

Bishop sucks in a sharp hiss and pulls away, leaving me breathless.

"I'm…I'm sorry, I just…" He cups my cheek with his hand and swipes his thumb over my swollen lower lip. "If you can't find anything to focus on, think of that when you get nervous up there."

His smile widens to a sinful grin, and I'm lost in the deep lines at the corners of his eyes. He drops his hand, though his gaze never leaves mine as he adds, "Oh, and Willow, I dare you to tell that story up there."

I let out a playful scoff. "What are we, twelve?"

"If that's what it takes." He winks. Freakin' winks at me. "And for the record, Patrick is a fucking idiot for letting you go."

My jaw drops.

Without another word, he turns and strides toward the door and back into the party, leaving me standing there with a dumbfounded look on my face.

CHAPTER FOUR
Bishop

Citrus and mint.

I can still taste her if I close my eyes. Which I've done a few times since returning to my seat, reliving and committing every moment of our conversation to memory. Tommy, Jackson, and Norah are all seated, along with two of our other teammates and their wives. They all got a kick out of the fact I'd been locked outside in the cold. I conveniently left out the part where it was with Willow York and the fact she left quite the impression. Though, I'm pretty sure Jackson knows—observant fuck that he is.

I wanted to believe she was like Corrine—money-hungry and entitled to what she thought the world owed her—but from the moment she opened her mouth, she did nothing but prove me wrong. And the crazy part is, I'm ninety percent positive she has no idea what a breath of fresh air she is. One I could easily find myself obsessed with if I'm not careful.

Jackson pulls me from my thoughts as he leans over and whispers, "So, where's your jacket?"

As I said before, observant fuck.

I stifle a groan by sipping my drink and shrug. "You mean your jacket? I must have left it at the bar."

"Uh-huh." He muses, his watchful eyes studying my face for any hint of a lie. "So, that's not it over there on the shoulders of that blonde getting ready to walk up on the stage?"

My gaze snaps to the front of the room where Willow stands with her father, my coat still draped elegantly across her shoulders.

Damn, she looks good dressed in me.

"Nope, must be another guy's coat," I bluff, my eyes never leaving Willow. They search for any sign of panic aside from the nervous way she twists her hands in front of her.

I have no business giving a shit about her. I shouldn't want to protect her or find an excuse to kiss her senseless again, but here I am entertaining all the above.

I try to remember the last time I felt this way. Corrine had been intoxicating from the start, but it didn't feel like a lightning strike of a kiss or a ravenous hunger for more.

"Right," Jackson chides.

He doesn't believe me, and I have no doubt that the second he's able to get me alone, he'll give me the third degree about how I just filed for divorce and absolutely shouldn't be making puppy eyes at a woman I hardly know. One, who by all accounts, is very much off limits. Richard York might be one of the better and more involved owners in the league, but he's still our boss, and if things went sideways, it could absolutely affect my career with the Renegades.

He may be correct, but I've never been one to dwell on the past. I had my night of drunkenly wallowing on his back patio after everything with Corrine went down. I cursed her name, swore I'd never fall for another woman, and woke up snuggling Jackson in the guest bedroom. Norah thought it was hilarious. Which is why a few videos of my misery still make the rounds in our group chat, but that was that. I may not have mourned my marriage like most, but like my momma always used to tell my siblings and me: life isn't going to wait for you to be okay; you just gotta keep going. Which is probably why I'm more like a charging bull when it comes to red flags. I see them as a suggested caution, not something to stop you. No one is perfect, and if you walk away from every risky endeavor, you'll never taste victory.

Look at me becoming a damn poet in order to justify my actions.

"Bishop," Jackson warns when I don't immediately respond, but I'm too focused on Willow.

Fuck, I really do have a problem.

She inhales a steadying breath as the MC announces her and shrugs off my jacket, handing it to her father. With her head held high, she climbs the stairs and takes her place at the podium.

She's stunning.

From the moment I stepped out onto the terrace, I thought so. I might have been irritated that I had to fetch her, but even I couldn't deny her beauty. And that dress. Fuck. The way the dark emerald fabric drapes off her shoulders and dips at her waist, hugging every single one of her delicious curves, should be a fucking sin. She's elegance and grace with a hint of independence and hot mess. And that was before she opened her mouth. Once she did, I was a goner. She may have been raised a socialite, but nothing about Willow screams high maintenance. She's genuine, which is hard to find in my line of work.

Her fingers dig into the sides of the podium, and even though she's smiling, her eyes are wide with fear as they scan the room. She swallows hard, and when she introduces herself, the wobbles in her voice threaten to take over. "Thank you, everyone, for being here."

She's letting the room win.

I silently will her to look at me, and she does. Grinning, I mouth, *I dare you.*

Her cheeks flush, and the sheepish smile that creeps across her lips makes my dick twitch. She releases a weighted breath, and the death grip she had on the podium loosens. Her eyes never leave mine, allowing me to witness the moment she nods and lets go.

It's like watching a rookie's first home-run in the big show.

Willow captivates the entire room with the story she told me on the terrace, just like I knew she would. It's raw and real. Something I don't think these people get to see often enough. She views her nervous over sharing as a hindrance, but if she can learn to harness it like she is right now, she'll be unstoppable.

In short, she's brilliant.

"Bishop," Jackson whisper-yells, drawing my attention back to him.

"What?" I snap, my eyes still glued on Willow.

"I know that look, Bish. There are only two times you get it: right before you're about to enter a game where the odds are stacked against us and when you're about to jump headfirst into something stupid. It's your *I'm a competitive asshole and think I'm invincible,* look."

"Pshh," I scoff, letting his comment roll off my shoulders. "I don't have that look."

"It's the same look you got the night you met Corrine."

My body tenses.

Reluctantly, I peel my eyes from Willow and turn to scowl at Jackson. "That was a low blow, Jack."

His shoulders slump ever so slightly, and I can tell he hates to be the one to tell me. "I know, but I don't want to see you rush into the same bullshit again."

I guess we aren't going to wait for privacy. We're going to do this right now in hushed whispers with our teammates and half of Manhattan's social elite within earshot.

Great.

"So you're okay with me going out with the Rookie tonight and sowing my wild oats, but I meet a girl who genuinely catches my interest and I'm supposed to just ignore that?"

"No. I mean, yes." He scrubs his hand over his face and shakes his head. "Look, I say this because I care about you and I don't want to lose you again, but you need a break from the wrong women. If you want to fuck Willow York tonight, that's fine, but she's a hop, skip, and a jump away from the woman Corrine became."

"She's not like that," I reassure, but it's more for me than him. Willow said it herself that she thought all the people here were asshats. She wears Converse and has dreams of helping people.

"That's what you said about Corrine. What are you going to do when she's got you at these events every other weekend. Not to mention watching her vacation in the Hamptons all summer while you're sweating behind the plate across the country, trying to keep your head in the game." Jackson sighs and I register the hurt in his voice. He took the brunt of my anger where Corrine was concerned. I accused him of trying to ruin my marriage, and yet he was the one who was there to always pick up the pieces every time she fucked me over.

I hate that he's right. Still, there's a part of me that wants to entertain the tiny voice in the back of my mind. Swearing Willow is nothing like Corrine.

Jackson gives me a half-hearted smile. "Look, I'm not saying don't spend the night with her. Just wash that struck stupid look off your face and take some time to enjoy being single. You haven't taken nearly enough time to heal after that bitch did a number on you."

"Is that you or your psychologist wife speaking?" I snort and instantly regret it.

Jackson glares at me, confirming what we both know. He's jumped from being my best friend to being Norah's messenger. She's probably also told him that I crave love because I was always searching for it at home. Being one of eleven, there's a lot of love going around. It's just never solely yours.

Yeah, I've got my own therapist who has similar opinions. I just don't see the problem with wanting to love and be loved.

He lets out another sigh and shakes his head before meeting my gaze with nothing but the love of a brother in his eyes. "I dare you to give yourself this year to enjoy this fresh start."

I. Dare. You.

With those three words, all the tension falls away and we're back to being Jackson and Bishop: best friends and teammates who aren't above playing dirty.

I shake my head. He knows I'm competitive as fuck, on the field and off. It's how I get the rookies to take risks. It's my signature move. The same one I used on Willow.

Jackson chuckles. "Wipe that sad look off your face, Law. You might find being single is not as bad as you think."

"Says the man who has the perfect wife." I huff.

"Hey, she shits just like everyone else."

I give him a pointed look and finish off my whiskey. "You are such a romantic."

"Nah, I'll leave that to you."

One year relationship free.

It's not the worst idea. And it doesn't mean I can't find out if Willow's pussy tastes as delicious as her lips. It just means I can't obsess and possess until she's mine like I usually would.

My heart protests, willing me to believe Willow is not like any other woman I've met so far, but I ignore it. Jackson's right. I can't remember the last time I wasn't chasing a woman.

"One year."

He nods and extends his hand between us and the table. "One year."

"Deal"—I put mine in his and shake it—"but then you have to help me find the right one."

"I'll put an ad out in the newspaper and host the Renegades version of *The Bachelor*, if that's what it takes."

I can do one year, but that year would have to start tomorrow because I've already decided I'm going to do whatever it takes to make Willow York mine for tonight.

41

NEW YORK

CHAPTER FIVE
Willow

"I'm so proud of you, Willy." My dad presses a kiss to my temple. "You've outdone yourself."

"Thanks, Dad." I beam excitedly, even though he knows how much I hate that nickname. Right now, I can't even find the will to berate him for it. I feel lighter than air and that's not just because he's twirling me around the dance floor like a princess.

Dad pulls me back in, and I furrow my brow while maintaining a playful smile. "Maybe next time don't mess with my seating chart?"

He chuckles and my smile spreads. I almost ask him to double-check the numbers, because it doesn't feel real. It was like I blacked out up there, and by the time I finished, everyone was on their feet clapping and willing to double their donations. We raised enough money on donations alone to finish building Camp Renegade Hearts, and if the projections from the silent auction are correct, we'll have enough to sponsor over a hundred kids for the summer and hire more staff for classes at our rec center in the city.

He gives me a shrug and winks as only dads can. "Eh, it worked out for the best. Plus, after that speech, you could have thrown the chart out the window. I—" He blinks, his eyes brimming with tears, something that never happens to Richard York. "I know things weren't always easy, and I haven't always been the best father, for which I am sorry. You are more incredible than I ever give you credit for. I love you, sweetie."

I blink away tears of my own. We've been close for years, but I've never shared with him how hard those moments were for me after my mother died. To have him not only hear me but recognize and apologize is everything.

"I love you too, Dad."

The string quartet finishes their song and my dad tugs me against him for another hug. "Now, I'm going to go find myself another scotch. You have fun tonight. You deserve it, Princess. This is your year."

My year.

I like the sound of that.

For the first time in a long time, I feel hopeful that despite everything my life is heading in the right direction. I don't need Patrick on my arm or the unattainable approval of my dead mother. I am finally making my own future.

My father presses another kiss to my temple and saunters toward the bar. I chuckle when he doesn't make it two steps without someone stopping him to chat.

That's my dad. He knows how to make everyone feel like they are the most important person in the room, and so, in turn, he's everyone's favorite person.

Making my way to the edge of the dance floor, I slide my phone out of my pocket to call Leighton and Indie. I need to check in with them and see how Leigh and the baby are doing, and tell her the good news. Only I'm greeted by the black screen and the memory of it dying and leaving me stranded outside.

Oh, crap.

Bishop.

I crane my neck and lift on my tiptoes to scan the crowded room. I have to find him, thank him, and give him his jacket, which is still lying on a table by the stage.

My elation is as much about him as it is about meeting our goal for the night. Maybe it was his mantra or maybe it was the way he believed in me when I couldn't, or maybe it's just the magic of the new year. All I know is that was the best speech I've ever given, and I have Bishop to thank for it.

I'm almost to the stage when an arm wraps around my waist and sends me violently spinning. Immediately, I'm assaulted by the smell of fish and cheap cigars. My stomach threatens to revolt, and I don't need to look up to know whose chest I have the displeasure of leaning against.

Albert Rojas.

At sixty-two, he's still considered one of New York's most eligible bachelors. He's easy on the eyes if you're into white hair, wrinkles, and old money. Which I'm not, but allegedly he was just my mother's type.

When I was sixteen, I found my mother's diary in the attic, and—let's just say, I know more about Albert's balls than I ever wanted to. Not that he has any idea, and I want to keep it that way.

However, my mother cheating on my father is not the part that makes my skin crawl. It's the fact that every time I see him at one of these functions, he never fails to proposition me. At first, Albert was an old man sweet, like when your friend's grandpa offers you a Werther's Original from his pocket and asks about your day. Over time, it became increasingly more creepy. Lingering stares became soft touches. Until one night, after a few too many, he asked if I'd like to join him and learn about the birds and the bees.

I nicely told him to fuck off, but that hasn't stopped him from seeking me out every chance he gets. Apparently, for him, no means *yes* and fuck off means *yes, please, I'll have another.*

Albert slides his hand inappropriately low on my hip as he turns and leads me back toward the dance floor. Which I allow because I don't want to cause a scene.

He leans in and whispers against the shell of my ear, "I hope you saved this dance for me, *mon chèri.*"

My limited knowledge of sophomore French tells me he means *ma chère,* but I'm not about to correct his pretentious ass.

His foul breath—a more potent version of his gag-inducing aroma—wafts across my face. A shiver wracks my body, and I swallow the bile that threatens at the back of my throat.

My eyes dart back and forth, looking for anyone I recognize to get me out of this situation, but find only those who would turn a blind eye to their old friend. "I'm actually on my way to find someone, Albert, but thank you for coming tonight."

I offer him a sweet smile—a far too kind gesture given his track record—but I'm not trying to cause a scene.

"Ah, come on, *mon chèri,* one dance won't hurt," he slurs with his fake French accent. The drunker he is, the thicker it becomes. I'm not sure what the story is behind it, but I'd say given the fact his words are slurring like he's been strolling down the Seine with a bottle of wine at his lips, I'm in store for at least an ass grab. Maybe an accidental boob graze, if not a full-on grope.

Albert's grip tightens on my hip like the panic in my throat, while his other hand forcefully guides me toward the center of the other couples dancing. They all stare from the corner of their eyes, too proper to intervene.

The sad part is I'm not surprised.

"Really, Albert, I can't right now." I try to reason, but he's already moving us with the music as his hand drifts to my ass.

"You wouldn't deny an old man his New Year's wish." He chuckles eloquently. "You look so beautiful. These child-bearing hips are more lush every time I see them. If I were twenty years younger, I would insist you give me an heir."

My lips part in shock.

In what world is that a compliment?

"Albert, I really—"

"But *mon chèrie*—"

"She said no."

His voice is menacing. My eyes dart over Albert's shoulder to find Bishop glaring daggers at the back of Albert's head from where he stands, blocking the flow of the other dancers.

I could kiss him for being the only one willing to intervene.

"Who the hell do you think you are?" Albert scoffs, a little spit dribbling from his lip.

"Her date."

Albert huffs. "Some date you are, leaving her unattended."

"She was dancing with her father, and I was ensuring she got a room upstairs so that we won't have to fight traffic to get home." The lie slips so easily from his lips, but all I hear is he was watching me. He knew where I was. What I was doing.

Heat fills my cheeks as I step clear of Albert's touch and croon. "Thank you, darling. "

In an instant, Bishop is there, wrapping an arm around my waist and tugging me into the safety of his arms. Flutters erupt low in my core.

Albert looks us up and down, his brow furrowed in uncertainty. "I didn't know you were dating someone."

It's a blatant lie. He'd met Patrick multiple times and conveniently forgot about him those times as well.

"Now you do," Bishop growls.

Albert's eyes search mine as if he thinks I'm going to stop Bishop's territorial barbarian act.

Not a chance in hell.

No man other than my father has ever taken a stand for me. They always choose to play the game. Bishop, on the other hand, couldn't give two shits. It was written on his face. The way his brow furrowed. The heat and annoyance in his gaze. This wasn't about appearances. It was about me. What I still didn't understand was why. Why did he kiss me? Why is he helping me?

Albert hesitates, his eyes darting back and forth before turning on his heel and leaving the dance floor.

A giddy smile tips my lips, and I glance up at Bishop, expecting to be greeted with a victorious grin. Instead, his jaw is tight and his eyes are still locked on pervy old Albert.

I reach up and circle my hand on his bicep. "Bishop?"

He winces slightly as if it physically pains him to tear his eyes from the bar where Albert now sits. By the time they reach mine, they've softened ever so slightly.

"Are you okay?"

"I'm fine, it's just Albert—"

Bishop shakes his head and growls. "Don't. Don't justify his actions."

"Bishop, I'm fine," I reassure him with a hand on his bicep before taking a step away from him.

We both hesitate, like neither of us wants this moment to end.

"Dance with me." It's not a question, but unlike when Albert asked, Bishop's request makes my core tighten and my knees weak.

I search his eyes, hoping to find a reason to turn and run. This isn't real. Fairytales don't exist, and Bishop isn't a white knight here to slay all of my dragons.

But what if he could? The tiny romantic that lives in the deepest parts of me counters. *Everything you've done tonight has been the opposite of what you usually do, and it's worked out well. What if this does, too?*

It's a compelling thought, one I shouldn't entertain.

"Bishop, I—"

"Willow, please." His voice is intense, barely a whisper. "Dance with me so I don't follow him and break every bone in his fingers for touching you when you clearly didn't want him to."

See? White Knight.

How is it one man can say all the right things? My heart is fragile, and my soul is riding the high of success, making it impossible for logic and reason to have a fighting chance.

For the second time tonight, I give in to Bishop and let go. He spins me in time with the music and catches me against his broad chest.

"You can dance?" I blurt out.

"Surprised?"

"Pleasantly. It's not every day that one meets a five-time all-star catcher, with an average that rivals the greats, and who can spin a girl around the dance floor."

Bishop raises a dark brow, and for the first time tonight, his smile reaches his eyes. "*You* follow baseball?"

It's devastating and panty-dropping all at the same time.

"Surprised?" I counter, echoing his confidence.

"Incredibly." He leans in, pressing his chest to mine and I feel every beat of his racing heart. His breath tickles my ear as he whispers, "What other secrets are you hiding behind that smile?"

"Nothing of consequence," I tease, knowing full well I'm walking a dangerous line with my flirtations.

"Oh, see I disagree. I believe there are many delicious secrets in that beautiful mind of yours." He pulls back just enough so that he can press his forehead to mine, halting our waltz. His gaze darkens and our breaths tangle, tangible as the tension between us. "And I'd like to explore them."

"Bishop, I don't think that—"

"Don't finish that statement. Don't tell me all the reasons I should walk away right now. I promise you I've already contemplated each one— and while they are all valid—I keep coming back to one solution."

"And what's that?" I ask, my voice a breathy whisper.

"Tonight."

"Tonight?"

"One night where we can be nothing and everything. Where you can let go and know I'll catch you."

Logic begs me to protest, but my heart wants to know more, even if it is a terrible idea.

"And what about you? What do you get out of this?"

Bishops leans in. His lips brushing so lightly against mine as he speaks, I question if it's real. "A taste of the most beautiful, intriguing woman I have ever met."

Me. He's talking about me.

Heat fills my cheeks and I smile and bite back the need to ask him if he's had his eyes checked. Instead, I manage to scrounge up one last ditch effort to thwart this reckless plan of his. If only to save myself from the comedown in the morning. "I just broke up with my boyfriend. I can't."

"I just filed for divorce last month."

"You're my father's player."

"The season hasn't started."

"I don't—"

He brings his finger to my lips and halts my protest as the song ends.

"I'm not here to convince you, Willow. I want you for tonight, but the choice is yours and always will be." He tucks a stray curl behind my ear, his fingertips leaving tingles in their wake. "I'm going to walk away now and refill my drink. Then I'm going to head upstairs to room twenty-four thirty-seven. You've got fifteen minutes to decide."

"You're the most impulsive person I've ever met."

"Maybe, but from where I'm standing, it looks like you could use a little more impulsivity in your life."

I stand there with my mouth parted and my heart thundering against my ribs as he turns and walks away.

My reasons are sound for why I should cut my losses and not look back. Despite wanting him, the bottom line is this isn't me. I may be the epitome of a hot mess, but I plan for that. I'm cautious and calculating. From the moment Bishop Lawson entered the narrative, he's been a wild card I didn't account for. I couldn't. But something he said resonates deep within me.

Let go for one night knowing I'll catch you.

My thighs clench and warmth erupts low in my belly. No one has ever bothered to catch me, but in one night, Bishop has proven he's a safe place to land.

One night.

I could do that and then tomorrow, reality would take over again.

New year. New me. New plans.

But first, I need to stop by my room. If tonight is about living with reckless abandon, I'm not about to let Bishop have all the fun

.

CHAPTER SIX
Bishop

I t's a miracle this suite was available, given the views—something about a cancellation and all they had left. I was too busy worrying I might have fucked up my chances with this grand gesture when I booked it.

My gaze scans the bedroom for the tenth time, lingering on the ornate art in brass frames and the sconces that probably cost more than the average rent in New York. Through the floor to ceiling windows of the bedroom, the famous New Year's ball sparkles, and all I can think about is if Willow will like it when I push her up against it and ring in the new year inside her.

If she shows up.

She's had ten of her fifteen minutes, and I'm still alone in arguably the nicest hotel room I've ever stayed in.

This is far from the most impulsive thing I've done for a woman, but it is the first time in a long time my heart has battered against my rib cage in anticipation. Jackson wasn't wrong when he called me out because this is absolutely me falling headfirst into a bad idea. It's me obsessing, possessing, and throwing caution to the wind for the sake of something that has the potential to feel real.

Fuck, I sound like an addict. And just like a junky knows the comedown is inevitable, I know full well my heart is going to hate me when reality streams in with the morning sun. But of course, that isn't about to stop me.

A soft knock sounds at the door, and I swallow hard, knowing once I open it there's no turning back.

I round the giant L-shaped sectional in the main room and open the door. To say my eyes light up is the understatement of the century. She's there. Standing before me, still in her stunning emerald gown with a sheepish smile on her face. She's got a small bag slung over her shoulder and her head tilted, allowing her curls to fall to the side.

Fuck, she's gorgeous, and I'd bet she doesn't even know it.

Stretching an arm out, I lean against the door frame and cock a brow. My lips twist up in a devilish smile. "I don't know if I didn't make myself clear. You won't need whatever is in that bag because once I peel that dress from your body, the only clothing you'll be wearing is my shirt."

Willow snorts and slides under my arm into the suite. "I promise you're going to want what I brought," she says sweetly, dropping the bag onto the small table before crossing the room to the ornate bar in the corner.

After plugging in her phone behind the bar, she deftly pours herself a gin and tonic with a twist of lime. The air of confidence she's trying to portray mesmerizes me.

She might think she's fooling me, but I notice the way her hands shake slightly and how she won't meet my gaze for more than a second. I note the brave vibrato she forces and the way she chooses the words she thinks I want to hear.

Which I do. But I also want her to be confident when she says them.

A few paces behind her, I reach the table and pick up the small black bag. I'm surprised by the weight of it and the way it jingles when it sways.

Intrigued as hell, I look up with a raised brow. "What's in here?"

Willow's grip tightens on the glass. Her cheeks tinge a beautiful shade of pink. "Go on, take a look."

She takes a sip, and I have to remind myself to slow down. I want her naked. Bare before me. Wrapping her lips around my cock like she is that glass. But I don't know if she's ready for that.

Resting the bag in one hand, I slip the other inside.

My jaw drops as my brain struggles to register what I'm looking at. It's every filthy dream come true—colorful silicone, glass, metal, and is that an eggplant?

If I was waiting for a sign, this is it.

This woman is surely going to be the death of me. My cock twitches against my zipper. Any hope of letting her go flies out the window as images of her using each one of these toys flood my mind.

When I finally draw my gaze back up to her, she's nervously tapping her finger against her tumbler. "This is the bag of tricks your ex hated."

Her lower lip catches on her teeth, and she nods. "I planned a special night for Patrick tonight. I wanted…it doesn't matter what I wanted. I'm here now."

"Oh, but it does, Kitten." Her ex is a fucking idiot. This gorgeous, compassionate woman is a gift to mankind, and he let her go. There's no way in hell I'm making the same mistake.

Rifling through the bag, I take stock of every item: nipple clamps, two vibrators, a dildo and an anal plug. There's no way we'll be using all of these tonight, but I have a few ideas that will ensure she's screaming till morning.

The tapping increases on her glass, and she shifts, clearly uncomfortable. "I wasn't sure you'd approve, but I figured tonight is about embracing what I want as much as it's about spending it with you." Her voice quivers with a vulnerability I find incredibly sexy. The way she articulates what she needs, even if she's afraid to ask for it.

I swallow hard so my voice won't betray my salacious thoughts. "Have you used everything in this bag?"

"Not everything." She hiccups.

In three strides, I eat the space between us. I need to be close to her for this conversation. If she wants this, I need her to feel the gravity of my words.

Willow backs up until her shoulders meet the cream-white wall, nowhere to escape.

I drop the bag on the bar behind me and cage her in with my arms on either side of her head. A tiny whimper slips from her, and when she tips her head back, I expect shock and maybe a little fear. Instead, there's nothing but heat in her gaze. I lick my lips. "What is it you want tonight, Willow?"

"You," she breathes.

Her answer would suffice for most men, but I'm not most men. If I only get one night with her, I intend to give her not only what she wants, but what she needs. The things she's only ever dreamed up in her fantasies. I'll commit to memory the way she sounds when she comes around my cock, and then I'll walk away.

At least, that's what I keep trying to tell myself, even if it's a blatant lie.

I trail my fingers up her forearm, my gaze never leaving hers. "And?"

"I—I've never done this before."

"What? A one night stand?"

"No. I—I don't know if I'm riding the high of exceeding our goal, or it's the magic of the lights out that window on New Year's or the fact I was cheated on a few hours ago. And even though I should care I can't bring myself to because it's clear he never gave a shit about me." She halts her nervous ramble and inhales past her nerves. For a split second, I think she's going to call off the whole thing, but she continues, "This is new for me because I've always put everyone else first. I'm a product of my environment, a lady of a social class that's never catered to me or my wants. I'm not the picture-perfect debutant. I hate this dress, all this makeup, and the pretense that anything I said downstairs mattered. It's a game to them. The grass isn't greener with trust funds and exorbitant bank accounts. It's fake. Which is why I don't usually let people in. It's…it's safer that way. But you…you're…I'm….shit, I'm sorry. I'm rambling again."

"You're doing beautifully." Reaching up, I tuck my favorite stray curl behind her ear, knowing it will fall free again. "Everything you shared downstairs mattered. But what happens here isn't about them." My hand lingers on her cheek, and I graze my thumb over her lower lip. "Now tell me, what is it you want?"

She lets out a strangled laugh. "No one has ever asked me that before."

"And yet I want an answer."

A small smile works its way onto her face, and I can see the wheels turning. "I—I want to forget who I am for a night. I want you to use my body. I don't want to feel guilty for wanting more than just missionary with the lights off. I want to come first. Is that selfish?"

I smirk. "No, Kitten, that's as it should be."

59

A barely audible gasp fills the space between us, and though her eyes radiate innocence, I know better. She's got claws.

"Really?"

I nod and wrap my hands around the glass, still in her hand. Taking it from her, I deposit it on the bar just behind me. "Do you trust me?"

"I don't know you. But for tonight, yes."

I ignore the qualifier of time because I'll take what I can get. My hand tips her chin enough that her red lips part below mine. Our breath mingles, and I swear sparks dance between us.

Desire. Lust. Unspoken Fantasies.

I nip her lower lip and savor her sharp intake. "If, at any point, there is something you truly don't want to do, Kitten, say so. Say the words and everything stops. Understand?"

Eyes wide, she nods.

"Words, Willow."

"I understand."

"Atta girl, because I want to give you everything you need. I want to push you beyond your comfort zone. I want to make your body sing so that every new year, when you utter the words to 'Auld Lang Syne', you remember this moment. I'm going to fill your ass with that plug and press you up against that window as the ball drops and fuck you hoarse. But first, I'm going to make you come again and again and again, so that you'll never doubt you should always come first."

Her eyes flash with something I can't quite place, and she presses her thighs together. Her hair falls from where I tucked it behind her ear, and before I can react, she rolls onto the balls of her feet and crashes her lips to mine.

I've experienced many kisses in my past, some great, some tragic, but none of them compare to kissing Willow York. She tastes the way a grand slam feels. Infinite.

My tongue sweeps between her lips, demanding entrance, which she gives me all too willingly. Juniper and lime explode on my taste buds, and the moan that rips from her throat sends a zap of lightning straight to my balls.

Her sounds are so damn sexy. And they're all for me.

One of her hands tangles in my hair while the other moves to my waist, pulling me flush against her. I know she can feel me. How hard I am. How much I crave where all this is going.

A shiver tears through her when I grind my aching cock against her core, and I can't help the smile that tips my lips. "Tell me, Willow, if I put my hands between your thighs, am I going to find you wet for me?"

She shifts, likely testing my theory, and whimpers a soft, "Yes."

I trace my fingers along the swell of her breast, down to the hollow of her waist, only stopping when I reach the top of the slit in her dress. She sucks in a sharp breath when I slip beneath the fabric, and I groan. Of course, she's wearing lace underwear. There's no way she could have known lace on a woman is my kryptonite, but it's par for the course when it comes to Willow.

My hand explores further, delving between her legs, sliding the thin fabric to the side. My fingers part her pussy lips, and I slide them through her slit.

"Fuck, Kitten, you're drenched."

My forehead drops to hers, and she hums her appreciation as she rolls her hips forward, silently demanding I play with the gift she's given me.

There's my little minx. She might be hesitant to ask for what she wants, but there's no doubt she knows, and I want her to have it all.

I slide against her, gently circling her clit, and I swear I can feel her pussy pulsing already. My other hand drifts to her neck, and her pulse pounds beneath my fingertips. The tempo matches mine.

I tighten my grip on her throat, at the same time I plunge two of my fingers into her soaked pussy. The needy little moan that escapes her lips, followed by a string of unintelligible pleas, undoes the little control I have left. I need her to come more than I need my next breath.

"You like that? My fingers in your cunt and around your throat," I say with a growl, tightening them further for good measure.

"Please, Bishop," she begs, and I'm taken with the way my name sounds on her swollen lips. The need to hear it again is all-consuming.

"Please, what, Kitten? Tell me what you want." I give her clit a little friction with my palm, and she pulses around me.

"Fuck," she whimpers, "I'm so close, don't stop."

Stop? I can't fucking stop. I couldn't even if I wanted to. Her body. Her mind. She's like a damn drug, and I haven't even fucked her yet.

As it is, I'm worried I'll come in my pants like a twelve-year-old boy from her pussy clenching around my fingers. I'll be lucky if I don't turn into a two-pump chump when she shatters around my cock.

Her moans pull me back, and I up the tempo of my thrusts, meeting those of her hips.

"That's it, Willow. Ride my fingers. You're such a good fucking girl, taking what you want." I lean forward, and nip her lower lip and rasp, "What you need."

She tightens around my fingers, and I know she's on the edge, ready to explode.

"Yes," she chants, her nails digging into my shoulder blades through my shirt. "Bishop, I'm—"

"That's it, Kitten," I croon. "Come for me, so I can find out just how sweet you taste."

"Ahhhh—God—" Her body tenses everywhere, her pulse thundering, and then, like a wave cresting, she crashes down.

She tips her head back and cries out my name, her body a mix of shivers and trembles. It's all I can do to hold back my release as she rides the current of pleasure coursing through her.

Fuck me, she's beautiful when she comes.

When she goes slack in my arms, I free my hands from her throat and cunt and wrap them around her waist, keeping her upright. As soon as I'm sure she's stable, I bring the hand still wet with her pleasure to my mouth. Her eyes widen when I don't bother to suppress my groan as I lick them clean.

"You're a dream," I purr.

The taste of her pussy has the same effect as stepping out of the dugout in full gear against our greatest rivals. I'm ready to go to war, my whole body demanding nothing short of a win.

Willow swallows hard and smiles. "That was…"

"Yeah—" my smile twists into a wicked grin "—and we aren't even close to done."

CHAPTER SEVEN
Willow

That twinkle in his eye is dangerous in the best possible way, and here I am without a single ounce of self-preservation left. If that orgasm is anything to go off of, I'm ready to run past all the reasons I shouldn't and drown myself in him.

Don't get me wrong. I've taken care of myself plenty of times, and occasionally Patrick and my previous boyfriends got me there. But none compare to the pleasure Bishop pried from my body. His fingers around my throat—paired with his filthy mouth—transcended space and time, taking me over the edge and beyond. It's more than I could have imagined, and yet it's exactly what I secretly hoped for.

Ever the gentleman, Bishop turns around and reaches for a bottle of water from the bar. Unscrewing the top, he offers it to me.

"Drink."

My gaze darts from his face to the bottle and back. I open my mouth to argue *I'm fine*, when he stops me with a glare.

"I see you ready to argue with me, but there are more orgasms to be had, and I can't have you getting dehydrated on me. Now drink."

Eyes narrowing, I take it from him and down half the bottle. Maybe I did need it. Not that I'd say that out loud. Allowing someone to take care of me is a new concept. The thought has always made me cringe. Hell, I don't even let Leigh and Indie do so, and they're my best friends. And yet, that's exactly why I showed up tonight. I'm tired. So fucking tired of being the one who holds everything together.

"Atta girl."

What is it about those two words uttered from his lips that make my thighs clench? I've heard "atta boy" muttered and chanted at the ballpark my entire life, but coming from his mouth is nothing like that. Bishop's praises feel genuine with a hint of filthy pleasure, and I crave them. I want to be his girl.

No. Not his.

Where did that thought even come from? This is about me. Not him. Not us.

When he's satisfied I've had enough, Bishop takes the bottle from me, sets it on the bar, and grabs the bag of toys.

My stomach flips, confidence wavering, and a seed of doubt blooms deep in my gut. Maybe I shouldn't have brought it. It's one thing to allow him in, but another entirely to give myself over in order to explore the kinks I've only ever entertained in my mind.

When he opened the bag earlier, I half expected him to be like every other man—intimidated by what they don't understand. I was wrong. So wrong. Bishop isn't a frat boy fumbling his way around a pussy because he never took the time to ask what a woman likes. He promised to make my body sing, and holy hell, he'd delivered. And that was just with his fingers. He didn't need the teammates I'd so willingly provided him in an effort to explore my own pleasure. I'll be lucky if I survive till midnight, let alone morning.

Then again, death by orgasms doesn't sound like a terrible way to go.

Bishop extends a hand, and immediately I place mine in his, my eyes dropping to the wet spot on his thigh.

I did that to him.

Heat fills my cheeks—something that happens a hell of a lot more since meeting him. When I look back up at him, his lips are pulled into a devilish smirk, like he knows what I'm thinking. My pulse quickens. There's no way he knows how much I needed this. I'm not even ready to admit just how much.

His silence as he leads me into the bedroom only adds to the anticipation brewing low in my belly.

Lights from Times Square filter in through the floor to ceiling windows, casting an iridescent glimmer. Neon dances over every surface, giving the ornate vintage comforter and stuffy nineteen-twenties painting a vibrant glow-up. It might be because it's New Year's, but there is a palpable charge in the air. Or maybe it's just the sexual tension.

I slip my hand from Bishop's and move toward the ensuite bathroom, but only make it two steps before he blocks my path.

"Where do you think you are going?"

"To clean up."

"I don't think so, Kitten." My core tightens at the use of his nickname for me. It makes me feel small, cherished, and somehow still sexy.

He reaches out his hand to me once more and beckons me to follow him. "Come here."

I'm helpless to do anything but obey.

When we reach the enormous bed, he spins me around to face the window. Then he steps forward, nestling his erection against me, and I have to chew my lip to stifle the groan in my throat.

His lips find their way to the exposed flesh on my shoulder, and he trails kisses up the crook of my neck until he reaches the shell of my ear. "If you think I'm going to let you wash away the pleasure that is rightfully mine, you're dead wrong." His fingers clasp the zipper just below my shoulder blades, and he lowers it until my dress falls away from my body and pools at my feet. "I'm going to savor every last drop like it's my last meal." He gently turns me so I'm facing him and adds, "And I'm starving."

I move to cover myself but halt when he shakes his head. His eyes trail down my body as if he's committing the sight of me to memory. It's intimidating, and I immediately fight against the instinct to snatch my dress back up and cover my imperfections.

"You're so fucking beautiful." His hands skirt the dip of my waist and flare of my hips, making my insecurities feel sexy. "I know you said you wanted more than just missionary with the light off. And I want to see every inch of you, but I love the way the neon dances across your skin with them off."

A filthy smirk crosses my lips as my hands trail down his sculpted chest. "I'm sure I would think so, too, if I could see it on yours."

"Is that what you want?"

That simple question captivates me more than a dozen roses ever could.

"Yes," I breathe.

"Is that your way of asking me to strip for you?"

I nod, and he gestures for me to sit on the bed.

It's a simple request. One I'm eager to obey, considering the reward is seeing Bishop in all his naked glory.

I lower myself toward the bed, but in my vain attempt to be graceful, my foot catches on my dress, and I stumble back onto the mattress. Flustered, I lay back so I'm resting on my elbows, looking up at him.

I expect him to laugh at my fall, but Bishop is nothing if not a picture-perfect Southern gentleman.

His gaze rakes over me as he slowly untucks his shirt from his slacks and begins to unbutton it from the top down. With each flick of his fingers, my eyes roam over his newly exposed flesh. Each ripple moves effortlessly, like a poetic masterpiece being written—raw, intense, and perfectly synced. He's gorgeous, but what entraps me is the knowledge that Bishop's beauty is so much deeper than his appearance. He might be pretty to look at, but this man feels with everything he has.

It's something I don't understand.

By the time he's tugged his shirt free and reaches for his buckle, I'm squirming on the bed—a needy, anxious mess, ready to feel his skin on mine.

He yanks his belt open, and in one fell swoop, pushes his slacks and boxer briefs to the floor.

My jaw drops, and I don't know where to look.

His cock bounces against his abdomen, the length of it nearly to his belly button. The glint of four steel barbells on the underside of his shaft, paired with the colorful tattoos sleeving his leg, has my mouth watering.

I shouldn't be surprised my golden retriever has a hint of a bad boy side, given his filthy mouth and penchant for wrapping his hand around my throat, but I won't lie. It's a welcome surprise. One that only intensifies the ache between my legs.

Bishop wears a devilish grin as he steps forward and drops to his knees in front of me. He snatches both my ankles, and a squeak escapes me when he drags me to the end of the bed. His warm breath lingers over my soaked panties before he hooks his fingers in the waistband and rips them, sliding the fabric from my body with ease.

"Don't worry, Kitten, I'll buy you a new set," he says, flipping my knees over his shoulders.

My mouth opens to berate him for ruining a pair of La Perla underwear. I don't get a word in before his mouth is on me, and I'm moaning his name. If his fingers were talented, his tongue is a damn gold medalist.

He sweeps it over my sensitive clit, and I can't help but arch my back to get away from him. It's wishful thinking. I might as well hold a funeral for my clit because she's died and gone to heaven.

Bishop's hands take root on my thighs and force my legs wide, demanding I stay open to him.

"It's too much," I cry, squirming beneath him.

"Hmmm. You're perfect. The way you taste drives me insane." He slides his tongue inside and devours me before finding my clit again and giving it a hard suck.

A gasp tears from my throat, though it sounds like it could be my soul leaving my body.

"And the noises you make. Jesus, Kitten, I could come from them alone," he growls, sending shivers down my spine. "But right now, it's your turn. You're going to come for me, and when you do, it will be my name on your lips."

Come again? Right now? I couldn't possibly. I've never come more than once with a man. On occasion I've gone more than once on my own, but never this close. Usually, I have to get myself back in the mood. Work back up to it. I figured he'd eat me out, fuck me, and then we'd be done. I came first. That's all I asked for. I thought he was joking when he said I'd come again and again. His words were supposed to be foreplay, not law.

My head shakes back and forth. "I can't."

"You can, and you will," he muses between the lazy circles he traces on my clit, and I hear the telltale jingle of my bag of tricks at his side.

My stomach simultaneously flutters and drops out of my ass when he stops touching me with his mouth and lifts my smallish metal butt plug with an emerald jewel at the end.

He turns the plug over between his fingers, examining it thoroughly but lingering on the jewel. "You looked stunning draped in this color tonight, but I think seeing it nestled between your impeccable ass will solidify it as my new favorite color."

I didn't think my cheeks could turn any pinker, but they did.

"Have you ever used this before?"

I nod as I prop myself back up onto my elbows. "Once on my own."

"And? Did you enjoy it?"

I shrug. "I started to, but then I got scared and didn't get it all the way in." It hurt too much. I wasn't sure if it was something I did wrong or if I maybe didn't have enough lube, but I stopped. And when I told Patrick about it, he told me that was disgusting, so I never tried it again.

"Can we change that tonight?"

He won't force me, but the challenge is there. The unspoken words—I dare you. Trust me.

And I do.

"Okay," I rasp, no wavering or uncertainty in my voice.

I watch the light dance across his lust-filled irises. It makes my stomach roll with anticipation. "Thank you for trusting me, Willow."

71

Willow.

Not Kitten.

He leans forward and kisses just above my clit. "Now, lay back and relax. Wrap your legs around my head if you must, but you're going to come again, and when you do, I promise you won't even notice the emerald in your ass."

Damn him and his mouth. The man holds nothing back. Both the words he speaks and his talented tongue. I don't think he knows how to. On the field and in the bedroom, never let it be said that Bishop Lawson gives anything less than one hundred percent.

Once again, his lips devour me. Savoring each swipe like he's a starved animal. It's no surprise I've been reduced to a writhing mess beneath him. Somewhere beyond the flicks and licks on my clit, I register the flip of the lube cap, followed by the cool press of his finger against my ass. It's foreign and uncomfortable, but he does an excellent job distracting me. Keeping me on the edge with his tongue, Bishop slowly breeches me, working his lubed finger in and out. Stretching me in ways I never knew possible.

The dual sensation of his lips and finger leaves me feeling like I'm losing my mind. It's uncomfortable, and I wince, my muscles protesting the intrusion. But that only lasts a moment before there is nothing but pleasure.

"Fuck, you're such a good girl," he praises. "You look so pretty, taking my finger in your tight hole. I can't wait until it's my cock instead."

We both know that's not happening tonight, but the sentiment of a next time warms a part of my heart that shouldn't be involved in this single night of debauchery.

He adds a second finger, stretching me until I moan, and just like before, the pain fades to ecstasy. His pace quickens, his fingers thrusting while his tongue wrecks me, flicking and sucking, leaving me more desperate for him.

My core tightens, and I swear the tip of my clit starts to tingle. It's light at first, but as his tongue continues to work double time, the sensation spreads further until my whole body hums with the need to come.

"Right there—oh God—Bishop—I'm going to—"

"Yes, Kitten," Bishop growls against my clit, and my hands fist the sheets. "Come all over my tongue. Let me taste you."

"It's—" I choke out.

It's what? My brain short circuits. It's too much. It's not enough. It's everything I shouldn't want, but holy hell, it's fucking perfection.

My legs tighten around his head, and I try to move my overstimulated clit away from his tongue, but when I move, he does, too.

An amused hum rumbles in his chest, and I can almost feel him smiling against me, my pain bringing his sadistic heart pleasure.

Bishop continues pushing me toward the edge, and just before I think I'm about to fall, I feel the cool metal of the plug pressing into me.

My mouth gapes, and I try to form coherent thoughts, but all I'm able to mutter is a slew of nonsensical curses and praises. My body shakes, clenching around the plug as he continues to suck my soul through my clit.

And then I let go.

"Fuck yes, Kitten. You're so fucking perfect, coming on my face."

"Yes—Bishop—coming—me."

Holy shit. I can't even form sentences.

My body goes limp, sagging into the bed, my mind floating in post-orgasmic bliss.

Bishop chuckles and places a kiss to my inner thigh before standing and giving me what's quickly becoming my favorite expression. The one where I'm everything right in the world. It feels like I'm his.

Wait. That's not right. One night only.

I slam my eyes shut, and there's a twinge in my heart begging for me to examine, but I push it away. It doesn't matter that he's piqued my interest or he's everything I should want in a man.

When I open my eyes again, I watch as Bishop disappears into the ensuite, and listen as he washes his hands. He returns with a grin, his eyes immediately falling to the plug in my ass.

I instinctively clench around the foreign object, and a jolt of pleasure tears through me, setting off a wave of shivers.

He huffs a throaty laugh. "How do you feel?" He offers me his hand and pulls me from the bed against his chest.

"Like I might float away if it wasn't for your hands."

His hand tangles in my hair and tips my head back so his lips can capture mine. He still tastes like me—warm and tangy—and I shouldn't find that as sexy as I do.

"It's a good look on you," he says, his cock twitching against my belly.

My post-orgasm bliss fades, replaced by guilt.

This man made me come twice without a single complaint while he's still painfully hard.

That just won't do. My mom may have done a lot of things wrong, but she didn't raise me to be ungrateful.

Intent on rectifying the situation, I reach between us and wrap my hand around him.

Bishop hisses and quickly covers my hand with his.

I look up at him and frown when I see he's giving me that downright sinful grin of his.

"It's almost midnight," he says as if that somehow explains why he stopped me from stroking him.

"But what about you?"

Bishop twirls a strand of my hair around his pointer finger before tucking it behind my ear. He follows his hand, leaning in until his lips tease the spot where my pulse thunders.

"Don't you worry your pretty little head," he croons and nips my skin. "I plan to wreck that tight little cunt of yours, but I figured you'd want to see the ball drop."

It's on the tip of my tongue to tell him I grew up in New York and have seen the ball drop almost every year since I was born, and I'd much rather explore the silver balls on the underside of his cock with my tongue. He silences me with a searing kiss that leaves me breathless.

"Let me rephrase that. I want to see the ball drop with you. Then I'm going to steal your first kiss of the new year and fuck you against that window like I promised."

My pussy clenches, and I let out a whimper as the plug jostles deep in my ass.

Yes, please.

CHAPTER EIGHT
Willow

A ll it would take was one flick, one well-placed suck, and I'd fall apart for the third time.

Three.

Not that I'm complaining. In fact, I'm pretty sure Bishop has already wrecked me for any other man, and he hasn't even fucked me yet. Should I be so lucky for him to keep his promises, I might be liable to throw myself at his feet and demand he make me his on the side. His long-distance fuck buddy.

It's obvious I'm not thinking clearly—be that from the orgasms or the plug in my ass, I'm not sure.

Lying down, the plug added pressure, but standing and moving has me teetering on the edge. With every step, it brushes against nerve endings I've only ever imagined being explored.

"Goddamn, you're beautiful."

Halting in front of the window, I look over my shoulder.

Damn, he's pretty. Too pretty for the likes of me, but I'm not about to tell him the sheer sight of him leaves me stuck on stupid.

A myriad of neon colors dance over his skin, accentuating every deliciously defined muscle. It's truly unfair how he's the whole damn package—the looks, the confidence, the unwavering compassion. Not to mention, he's able to locate the clitoris, which honestly makes him a god among men.

"Like what you see?" Bishop interrupts my ogling, and I scoff playfully.

He crosses the space between us in three large strides and wraps his arms around me. His chin rests on my shoulder while his weeping cock nestles between my cheeks, pressing against the jewel of the plug.

I let out a hiss, and I don't miss the way he rocks his hips in response.

As practical strangers, standing together like this should be awkward, but somehow, with him it feels like the most normal thing in the world. There's a comfortable silence between us. A hushed promise of one night that's only enhanced by my tiny gasps and his thrusts as he continues to use his cock to jostle the plug to the faint beat of the music outside. We watch the crowd below, packed together like sardines in order to witness one of the most iconic New Year's traditions in the world—one I've always taken for granted living in the city.

But not this year. Nothing short of a lobotomy will tear the memory of this moment from my mind.

"If you keep wiggling that ass of yours, we won't be watching the ball drop," Bishop growls.

"Me? You're the one rocking that monster cock of yours against that jewel like a genie is about to pop out of it."

"It is a very pretty jewel," he murmurs along the shell of my ear, eliciting a shiver that wracks my body. He buries his nose in the crook of my neck and runs his tongue over my pulse point.

My hips jerk back, and I lift myself up, giving him the friction he deserves. The friction I want so badly against my clit. "Please, Bishop," I pant.

Ten.

He ignores my plea as the crowd below us begins to count down. "Do you have a wish for the New Year?"

"Like a resolution?" I ask, arching my back and pushing my hips toward him. How can he be asking me something so mundane when he's firing up my libido like a damn hotrod?

Nine.

"No, a wish." His hands expand over my hips, his grip tightening so I can't move. He presses his lips to my shoulder, leaving a feather-soft kiss. "Your wildest dreams, Kitten. Something that falls somewhere between manifesting destiny and good luck."

Eight.

I wrack my brain for thought, but all I can think about is the impossible ache between my legs and the way his rocking against the plug is not quite enough to get me there.

"I…I wish—"

"No." He halts his movement, and I let out a mewled whine. "You can't tell me."

Seven.

"Then why did you ask?" I cry out in frustration.

Bishop chuckles against my skin and resumes his languid strokes. It's pure torture. "To make sure you have one."

Oh, I have many, I want to scream. *If you asked me two hours ago, I'd tell you all about them.* Each carefully constructed with a ten-point plan to achieve them. But right now, there is only one that comes to mind, and it's tied to the man asking the questions and my overwhelming desire to come.

Six.

"Do you have one?" I pant, trying to focus on his words instead of the metal fucking my ass, which is simultaneously too much and not enough.

"Absolutely," he purrs, and I can almost hear the smirk in his voice daring me to ask what it is.

Five.

The joke's on him. I won't be baited, and I'm tired of playing his game.

The next time he rocks back, I lean forward, severing our connection. Lifting onto my toes, I wait for his cock to bounce down and capture it between my thighs, sliding it through my slick cunt.

"Yessss," I moan as the tip of his dick hits my clit.

"Fuck," Bishop growls at the same time, his teeth digging into the flesh on my shoulder. "You don't play fair."

"I never claimed to," I rasp, thrusting my hips and using him to chase my pleasure.

Four.

"Condom," he grunts, stilling against me.

"Pill," I mutter clumsily. I am so close.

A low growl rumbles. "I'm clean."

"Me too."

"Fuck, you're perfect."

He teases my clit again with the tip of his dick. His hands cup my breasts, and his calloused thumbs brush the tips of my nipples with light flicks. Each one elicits a shallow inhale, followed by a soft mewl.

"Willow, look at me." His soft words have alarms sounding as I crane my neck and meet his dark, lust-filled gaze. "Play dirty all you want, but with me, all you have to do is ask."

Three.

This man. He's perfect. Fucking perfect.

Two.

A grin forms on my face. "Bishop. Fuck me."

"Just for you, Kitten."

His lips crash against mine as the crowd chants *one,* and a chorus of Happy New Year's erupts. There are fireworks and confetti with wishes for the new year scrawled on them. None of that matters because Bishop Lawson is kissing me senseless, and I'm living for the promise of what comes next.

In one swift motion, Bishop breaks our kiss, bends his knees, and hooks his hands through the inside of my legs, wrapping them around my thighs. He lifts and spreads me so I'm pressed up against the window and flashing the world my pussy.

"Happy New Year's, Kitten."

I only have a split second to freak out that he's going to drop me when Bishop thrusts upward and seats his cock fully, knocking the air out of me. It's like nothing I've ever felt before, and I don't know which sensation to focus on—the sliding of his piercings, the way his cock fills the deepest parts of me, or the plug that makes me feel like I might burst.

It's all heat and sweat as his balls slap against my clit, and the plug grinds at the apex of each thrust. Instincts take over, and I tighten around him, pulsing against his steel bars, bursting with pleasure. My skin tingles, and it's like I'm waiting for the tidal wave to pull me under.

"Fucking hell, Willow." Bishop grunts, followed by a few more curses.

"I can feel—shit—your pussy is so goddamn tight…and the plug… it's trying to force me out."

Panic floods me, and I open my mouth to tell him he better not pull out. Thrust harder, hug me, wrap me around his waist—I don't care what the hell he does, as long as he doesn't pull out. Only I say none of those things. All I can do is moan in pleasure.

"That's it, Kitten, keep going," he pants, his voice dark and dirty as he begins to thrust. Short strokes at first, allowing my body to adjust to the movement of both him and the plug in my ass. His fingers dig into my thighs, and I'm positive I'll have bruises and the outlines of his nails come morning, but I don't care. I'll wear his battle scars into the new year like a badge of honor.

Bishop moans, his thrusts becoming more forceful as he bounces me up and down the entirety of his length. The squats this man must be able to do to sustain this position is insane.

Fucking catchers.

I mewl softly, and my eyes roll back in my head when he hits a spot I've never felt. I'm not sure if it's because of the plug, his cock, or the fact that my orgasm never quite subsides—it just continues to build, like a tsunami gaining strength as it approaches land—but I know that when I explode, there will be no turning back.

As if there was a chance after I walked into the suite.

Never.

Bishop is going to do exactly as he promised. Except he's not only going to wreck me. He's going to ruin me.

The sound of "Auld Lang Syne" echoes outside while my insides start to splinter as his breathing starts to become choppier and more ragged.

"I'm close, Kitten," he grits out.

"Me, too," I manage, rolling my hips to meet his thrusts.

"Get yourself there. Play with that sexy little clit and come all over my cock."

His words stoke the flame of my desire, and I feel my impending orgasm start to take hold. Following his directions, I lean into the window, using one hand to keep me steady while I reach the other between my legs and stroke my swollen clit.

One swipe and a hard thrust from Bishop and I fall apart. The window catches me, the cool glass a welcome contrast to the heat wracking my body. My pussy flutters around him, my ass clenches around the plug, and it's all I can do to keep myself upright.

Bishop groans, and his thrusts become more erratic.

I'm still coming down from the high of my orgasm when he finishes, milking every last drop of come he has into my pussy.

"Fuck," he breathes and leans his forehead onto my back. "You come so beautifully."

"You're not so bad yourself," I pant, unable to come up with anything more profound.

Bishop chuckles and gently slips himself from me, sliding me down until my feet reach the floor. I wobble like a baby deer, but he's there to catch me. Because of course he is. Patrick never gave two shits about me after he'd emptied himself. It was always about cleaning up and getting to bed because he had an early morning.

Not Bishop.

He kneels behind me and presses me forward so my hands rest on the window, and with a soft touch, he tells me to bear down as he slips the plug from my ass. Then he's beside me, tugging me against his chest like that's the only place I belong.

And I'm beginning to think, maybe I do.

NEW YORK

CHAPTER NINE
Willow

I shake the dangerous thought from my mind and look up at the man who is rapidly carving a place in my heart despite my protests.

"Hi," he whispers with a lazy smile.

"Hello," I whisper back, unsure what else to say. I'm overwhelmed and overstimulated and trying to work out the warring emotions in my chest.

"Are you alright? That was…a lot."

"I'm good," I lie.

The truth is, I just need him to stop looking at me so I can figure out where I stand.

He tucks a finger under my chin, and his deep brown eyes capture mine with a steadiness that unnerves me. "Just good?"

His astuteness is a blessing and a curse.

Thank God my phone rings, effectively halting the conversation.

"I should probably get that," I murmur, awkwardly untangling myself from his arms.

He nods, but the concern in his gaze and the way he arches a brow tell me he's not fooled by my bullshit.

"I'm going to hop in the shower. Join me when you're done."

"I can just head back—"

He steps forward and presses a finger to my lips, silencing me. "One night."

"One night," I echo and watch as he heads toward the ensuite, giving me a view of his perfectly sculpted ass.

My phone stops ringing, and for a split second, I almost forgo checking who it was in favor of following him—until it starts ringing again.

I quickly enter the living room and see Leighton's name flashing across the screen. Immediately, I swipe to answer the video call. Bringing the phone up to my face, I angle it to shield my nakedness.

"Is he here?" I squeal.

"Happy New Year to you, too," she scoffs playfully, looking far too put together to have just pushed a baby from her vagina. But that's always been Leigh. Gorgeous in every situation.

She points the phone down, and the screen fills with the most precious baby boy. He's got a full head of blond hair like his momma and an adorable button nose, and ten tiny little fingers, three of which he's sucking on while he sleeps. "But yes, he's here. First baby born in the new year at Mid City General."

Tears well in my eyes, and I swallow past the sob in my throat. "Leigh, he's perfect."

She looks down at the little boy, who is now the center of her world.

"He is, isn't he?"

This tiny baby might be the result of a one-night stand that left Leighton with a lot more than she bargained for, but you'd never know it with how much he's already loved.

"What's his name?"

Her smile brightens her eyes, something I haven't seen from my best friend in a long time. "Zachary Lee James."

A tear slips free. "Your dad would love him, Leigh."

Her lip trembles. "I know."

Five years ago, Leigh lost her parents in a car accident. Everything was fine until her grandparents found out she was pregnant and unmarried. They disowned her because she wouldn't be able to fulfill the marriage they'd arranged for her.

It was some real uppity society bullshit that made me happy my mother was no longer alive. That's when I hired her as my CFO at Renegade Hearts. Not only is she my best friend, but she gets what it's like to live without a parent.

"Where's Indie?" I ask. She's the third in our epic trio and the only reason I didn't race to the hospital after the gala. That and the fact the hospital allowed only one support person in the room. It definitely has nothing to do with the naked man steaming up the shower in the next room.

"She's getting me food. It's absurd that they expect you to push a bowling ball through a bagel-size hole with no sustenance. But more importantly, where is your dress?"

My eyes dart to see the nip slip on the screen, and I instantly jerk the camera upward. "Uh...well, you see what had happened was..."

"Willow Mae York." She pretends to clutch her pearls and puts on her best high-society accent. "Who got you out of your knickers and into bed?

Because I read your texts, and I know it's not that cheating bastard Patrick, which we still need to discuss."

"It's no one," I blurt out defensively.

"Usually, I would believe you, but if I'm not mistaken, that isn't your apartment. Or the gala. Which I know is still raging on because I confirmed the DJ until four." She leaves off—but implies—I'm the prudish member of our little threesome, and while kinky, I'm not usually one for one-night stands.

Until tonight.

Fuck, what the hell was I thinking? She might not have outright said it, but Leigh's implications are spot on. This isn't me. None of it. I don't let people in. I don't fall into random stranger's beds. I plan galas and change the lives of thousands of kids. I hold my cards close to my chest because if you don't, people disappoint you. I don't give them the chance.

"Wait, Wills, isn't in her bed? Where is she? She's not a hit-it-and-quit-it girl, so I know she's not with a man."

Shit. Indie is a damn bloodhound when it comes to sniffing out information. She's not above paying someone to hack the hotel security cameras just to find out if a guy is cheating on one of her costars. I can't imagine the lengths she'd go to uncover my little secret.

I need to go. I need to get back to my room.

"I'll tell you guys all about it tomorrow," I stammer. "Give baby boy all the snuggles for me, and I'll be there in the morning. Byyyyyeeeee."

Leighton's smile widens, and I disconnect the call, knowing I'm in for a shit ton of questions tomorrow.

A heavy sigh heaves from my chest, and I succumb to the weight of my decisions settling over me like a bad rom-com. It's tragic, really. I'm a total cliche—the woman banging the gorgeous charismatic player on the baseball team her father owns, believing there's a chance for something more.

I set my phone down and head back into the bedroom, where my dress is still pooled on the floor next to Bishop's suit.

"Why does it look like you are contemplating putting that back on?"

His voice startles me, and when I turn, he's leaning against the doorframe with a towel wrapped around his waist and water gliding down the ridges of his abdomen.

My gaze drops to the floor, and I shrug. "I just thought it might be best if I left."

"Is that what you want?"

I shake my head and wince. I'm retreating, and he's still putting me first. I just wish for a split second he'd be an asshole. It would make walking away so much easier.

My hands fist at my side, a manic attempt at feeling in control. But before I can answer, my stomach lets out an absurdly loud grumble. My eyes go wide, and I look down at the offending organ.

"When was the last time you ate?"

"I'm fine. I'll get some food when I get back to my room." Picking up the bag of toys, I gather my dress in my arms. If I can just avoid looking at him and remembering all the great things about him, I'll be able to make it out of here.

His footsteps follow me as I make my way back into the main room and do a once-over to make sure I don't forget anything.

"Willow, when was the last time you ate?"

I roll my eyes. The man might withhold orgasms, but he couldn't be shitty if his life depended on it.

I fiddle with the fabric of my dress in my hands and try not to give in to the urge to glance at him through my periphery. "Uh, I had a few crackers for lunch and some hors d'oeuvres at the gala."

He lets loose a few muffled curses, and I look over just in time to see him run his hand from the base of his skull to his forehead and down his face.

"Shower. I'll order room service."

"Bishop—" I protest, finally finding the courage to meet his gaze.

Only it's a mistake.

When I walked into the bedroom after that call, I'd been ready to walk away. I forced myself to forget the way he made me feel and how hard he made me come. Because this isn't who I am, even if it is who I wish I could be.

With one look, though—one pleading stare—he's cracking my resolve and burrowing back in.

The problem is, if I let him, I'm not sure I'll be able to walk away. And I need to.

But when he looks at me, I almost believe he needs this as much as I do.

"Kitten." His voice shakes. "Please. One night. Suspend reality with me. Just you and me."

Yes. The word is on the tip of my tongue. I play a big game for the masses, but Bishop didn't get that girl. Because he caught me at my lowest, he's only seen the rawest parts I hide away on my best days. Which is why I know this is going to gut me when it's over. Because the truth is, I don't want to leave. I know it can't last. I know I'm going to get hurt, but I don't care.

I need this.

One night. For me. For him. For us.

"Okay." I nod and cross the space between us. When I reach him, I rock up onto my tiptoes and place a reassuring kiss to his cheek. To which he responds by gathering me into his arms.

We don't owe each other a damn thing, but there's something we both agree on. Neither of us is ready to let reality in.

So, we don't.

CHAPTER TEN
Bishop

I almost lost her.

Not that she was mine to begin with—a fact I still struggle to wrap my brain around.

I would have let her walk away if she wanted, but we both knew she didn't. Uncertainty came with the territory. It was something new. Something neither of us expected. And then reality came crashing into our little hotel sanctuary.

My heart seized when I heard the tail end of her conversation with her friends as they called her out for her actions. I had to choke back my protests. Even if they meant well, they pushed Willow into feeling guilty for what she'd done with me. That just won't do. Because that's the thing about friends. They know us inside and out, but there will always be a part of us we don't allow them to see.

The magnetic spark between us—I don't know if it can last, but I'm willing to chase it into the morning light.

I'm also completely intrigued by the person she lets her friends see and have every intention of getting to know her, too.

The sound of the shower echoes through the suite, but it's not enough to drown out the pounding of my heart against my rib cage. Jackson was right. I can't do casual. One night is never enough for my heart, even when I know damn well there are more red flags than at a Soviet parade. Most of which are my own.

I slip on the fluffy white hotel robe and call down to the front desk, ordering one of everything off the menu. Overkill? Absolutely. But I promised to take care of her, which means planning ahead. Plus, all the desserts here are amazing, and despite being an elite athlete, I am never one to turn down anything fried, dipped in powdered sugar, or drizzled in chocolate.

Images of licking chocolate from the tips of Willow's dusty pink nipples drift through my mind, and my blood instantly rushes south. Shit. The last thing I need is her walking out here to find me sporting a hard-on and thinking I want this to just be about the sex. Which, don't get me wrong, that part is phenomenal, but I truly want the rest of her, too. Even if it's just for tonight.

I flip on the TV and watch the highlights of the hockey game. Apparently, the Devils won in overtime. Normally, I wouldn't care, but one of my little sisters decided she wanted to fuck around and find out with their goalie, and now they're dating. Also, the game proves to be a great distraction and stops me from acting on my urge to lose the robe and join Willow in the shower.

She needed a little space, which I'm happy to give, even if I'd much rather explore all the ways I can make her come before dawn.

Yet the longer I sit here, the more my doubts creep in. Like I'm waiting for the other shoe to drop, and I'll look her up online and find out she's been arrested for throwing a bag of puppies into a river or something just as unforgivable.

Thank fuck the food shows up, so I don't have a chance to examine my answer to that dark thought.

Seconds after the bellhop leaves, I hear a tiny gasp and turn to find Willow standing wide-eyed in the bedroom door. A matching fluffy white robe covers her. I hope she didn't bother putting on anything underneath.

"Willow Mae," I tease, tipping my head in greeting.

She winces, but it does nothing to detract from her beauty. "You heard that, did you?"

My mouth twitches as I try, and fail, to hide my smile. "Family name?"

Willow falls against the doorframe and nods, her wet curls falling into her face. "Hazard of my father being a rabid baseball fan."

"Seriously?" His brow crinkles. "You're named after Willy Mays?"

She rolls her eyes, and I get the feeling she's told this story more than once in her lifetime. "The one and only. What other embarrassing secrets did you hear thanks to my best friends?"

"Just your name," I lie. "Your delicate image remains intact, Kitten."

"Delicate. That's one way of putting it." She huffs, pushing off the wall. "Listen, I'd rather not think about what society thinks of me tonight. Save that for the morning."

My brows knit together. She's a mystery of confidence and insecurity. One I'm ready to unravel and reassure. Then find out who hurt her and tear them apart.

But first, she needs to eat.

I lift my hand and offer her the feast I cultivated. "Shall we then?"

Her eyes go wide at the silver domes on every available surface. "Is this all for us?"

Uncertainty creeps in, and I wonder if I went too far. Not that she doesn't deserve it. She does.

I shrug and smile. "I didn't know what you wanted, so I ordered a little of everything."

"Of course you did." She shakes her head.

I don't know what the hell that means, but given her frown morphed into a grin, I'd say I did well.

"Can we start with dessert? Is that what I'm smelling?"

"Ugh." I close my eyes and tip my head back, letting an exaggerated moan escape. "Could you be any more perfect?" Lifting the dome of the tray on the coffee table in front of me, I reveal perfectly fried New Orleans-style beignets.

Her cheeks flush crimson, and I'm so focused on her embarrassment that I almost miss the dark flash of emotion that flits across her eyes. If I had to guess, she doesn't like being complimented, but that's too damn bad because there is no way in hell I'm stopping.

Willow forces a smile and joins me on the sofa, sitting right next to me instead of at the other end. Her shoulder brushes against mine, and I catch hints of her citrus smell paired with the sweet hotel shampoo. It's intoxicating. She leans forward and picks up the fried dessert. "My father always says life's too short not to have dessert first."

"He's a wise man."

Willow takes a bite and lets loose a soft moan before relaxing into the plush sofa cushion. It's a close second to my favorite sound. "It's just like New Orleans. You have to try this."

She offers me the beignet, only instead of taking it, I lean forward and take a bite directly from her hand, skirting my tongue across her fingers. Her gaze drops to her hand while flavor from the soft dough and powdered sugar explodes on my tongue. I usually prefer my fried dough in the shape of a circle with a hole poked out of the middle and copious amounts of frosting, but I can't deny this is one of the best things I've ever tasted. Especially with a hint of Willow York on the side.

"Your dad might be onto something—starting with dessert. There's no way I can be disappointed now if the steak is overcooked."

She tips her head to the ceiling and lets out a hearty laugh. "I'll have you know, anything more than medium rare is a sin."

"A girl after my own heart."

She smiles sheepishly, and for the next hour, we try bites of each dish and talk about nothing and everything. I kick my feet up on the table, and she settles into the couch with her legs tossed over mine. My fingers trace circles on her thighs as I tell her about growing up in the South, and she regales me with stories of growing up in New York, divulging all the dirt on the people I had the pleasure of meeting at the gala tonight. She tells me about her best friends, and they remind me of my college friend Grant, and of course, Jackson and Norah. The difference being baseball is what bound us and not a love of dirty books.

Her eyes light up when she talks about Leigh and Indie and their book club of sorts. "I used to bring the books home from school and read them in the owner's suite during the games that stretched on forever. Then I'd write a note about what I loved about the stories and send them to Indie or Leigh."

"Sisterhood of the traveling smut," I say with a laugh, knowing my sisters would love her for her reading preference alone.

"Exactly."

I bring my hand to my chest like I've been wounded. "Though, I'm hurt you didn't watch us play."

"You weren't on the team yet, so don't get your panties in a twist."

"I suppose it's better that way. Wouldn't want you getting all hot and bothered by any other Renegades."

"Never." She shakes her head and makes a cross over her heart, a solemn promise.

My brow raises, and I lean toward her, lowering my voice. "Is that where you got your inspiration for all those toys?"

Her lips purse to hide her smile. "A lady doesn't kiss and tell."

"We're past kissing, Kitten."

"They may have given me a few ideas over the years."

And fuck if I don't want to know every single one.

I swallow hard and grip her thigh, the tiny mewl she makes zapping my dick to attention. This is one of those proverbial crossroads that could easily lead us down a road that ends with me fucking her again and again. But then I wouldn't get to hear her voice. I wouldn't get to explore that beautiful soul of hers that turns me on as much as her cunt. If I only get her for one night, I want all of her.

I chew the side of my cheek, willing my hardening cock to behave as I one-eighty our conversation to safer waters.

"Are you close with him? Your dad?"

Willow tilts her head and furrows her brows like an adorably confused little kitten, but doesn't call out my shift in topics.

She shrugs. "Mostly. After my mom died, we were inseparable. When I went away to school, we drifted apart. Now, I'd say we have a typical father-daughter relationship. I'm his pride and joy, but always directly behind the Renegades. You guys are his purpose, his will to get up every morning. I'm sure you understand that. You don't just wake up and decide you're going to play major league baseball. You worked your ass off to get where you are."

I nod, considering her words. "Baseball has been my life since I was seven years old. It was the only time I got my dad to myself since my brothers were so much younger than me. Then I sort of just fell in love with the sport."

It was one hundred percent selfish, but it was the only thing that was mine. None of my brothers enjoyed it. They were the golden boys of our town, fielding our football teams from the tender age of five. But baseball was mine. There was just something about the sport, especially as a catcher. It's my job to protect my team. I'm their first line of defense, calling pitches and knowing the ins and outs of our opponent's lineup. It helps that it comes naturally to me.

"How many brothers do you have?" Willow asks.

"Four. And six sisters. I'm the eldest boy. Second oldest overall."

"Your parents must be saints."

I let out a playful scoff. "Or certifiably insane."

Willow pulls her legs from my lap and sits up straight. She leans forward, trailing her fingers along the hem of my robe at my shins. My eyes are drawn to where her rope parts, almost exposing her pussy.

I'm about to do my own exploring when her fingers brush over the eleven stars that surround the compass rose. "Are these for them? Your siblings?"

Her touch is light, but it might as well be lightning with the way it stokes the heat within me.

I suck in a short breath. "You're observant. Anyone ever tell you that?"

"It comes with the territory of being the quiet bookworm."

She gets a distant look in her eyes, and I get the feeling there is more to that sentiment.

"There's nothing wrong with being the smartest one in the room."

"I know. I just…brains were not appreciated by my mother." She winces past a measured smile, and I wish I could take away the pain in her voice. She hesitates. I wait for her to continue—but when she does—it's not to give me more of herself. "Do they all have meaning? Your tattoos."

"They do." I nod. "And for the record, your brain is the sexiest thing about you."

Tears rim her eyes, and she smiles. "Thank you, Bishop."

"Any time."

Her fingers trace the compass surrounded by roses. "What's this one for?"

"My parents. My mother's name is Rose, and she always said my father was the north star of our family."

Her featherlight touch moves to outline the thin, black ink of the soft pink ballet slipper atop a harp surrounded by violets. "And this one?"

"My sisters, Vivienne and Violet. They're twins. One's a prima ballerina, the other a harpist."

She follows the dots and smaller stars between the bigger art pieces to a slice of cake with a giant cherry on top and looks up questioningly.

"Sutton, the youngest. She's a baker."

"I shouldn't be jealous that you have tattoos for all these women, considering they are your sisters," she muses, never stopping her tracing, and I can't help but fill in the part I want to hear most.

But I am.

Her jealousy, even if it's only playful, is a step away from possessive, and I can absolutely live with that notion.

I roll my hips and turn so Willow has a view of the back of my calf and the rest of my ink. "And what would you have me get for you?"

"I'm not sure."

"Think about it," I tease. "There will be a quiz later."

She chuckles. "Why did you start getting them?"

"I wanted to take them with me no matter where my career takes me."

"That's sweet," she says thoughtfully.

Slowly, she moves to each of the inked memorials in my skin, listening intently as I explain each one. A guitar for Joel...a ship for Charli...a paper airplane for Bri.. and so on and so forth, until she knows the story of each of my siblings. Most women ask about them, but they don't care. They don't hang on every word like they are committing it to memory. Willow does.

The tips of her fingers trail up and circle the bees and honeycomb on my knee. "And what about this?"

I can't help the laugh that booms from my chest. "That was a lost bet with a college teammate."

Willow's brow raises, and I can see the wheels turning as she tries to figure out what could possibly entice me to get such a tattoo.

"I had to prove forever that he's the bee's knees."

She tips her head back and laughs, and I swear it's the most magical sound I've ever heard. What's that thing they say about people laughing and fairies getting wings? Well, Willow's laugh could give flight to an entire army of fairies.

When she gains some semblance of composure, she wipes away a tear. "Do I even want to know what the bet was?"

"That's the thing. We were both drunk so neither of us remember exactly what the bet was, only that it solidified our friendship. A few years later, he got the same tattoo."

She grins at me. "Awww. There never was a sweeter bromance."

"Don't let Jackson hear you say that." The truth is, Jackson and Grant get along better than I'd ever hoped. For a long time, I worried they wouldn't click, but when we were all chosen for the All-Star team a few years back, they took it as a chance to gang up on me and ensure I never forgot just why they were my best friends.

"You guys are really close, aren't you?"

"Jackson's the brother I chose in New York and if you ask my mom, Grant is a Lawson."

Her eyes soften and match her almost wistful smile. "I love that for you."

I swallow the emotions clogging my throat. It's such a simple sentiment, and it's so Willow. She's not the kind of girl who wears her heart on her sleeve like I do. She's been raised in a world where she's had to fight to be herself, and yet, she's still able to be genuine with her words.

Her touch pulls me from my admiration as it pushes the bottom of my robe higher. "If your lower leg is for your family, what's on the upper half?"

"That space is reserved for the moments that changed my life."

She arches her brow. "The plot thickens."

It's not the only thing thickening, but I don't bother telling her that. If she continues this little expedition of hers, she's going to be greeted by more than ink. As it is, I'm having a hard time keeping the fabric of the robe from making it too obvious I'm more than a little hard.

Her eyes lift to meet mine, and I grin wildly. "Is that your way of saying you're reading my skin like one of your dirty books?"

"Depends. Is there a happy ending?"

This woman. I'm trying my best to show her I want more tonight than just her body so when morning comes I've got an iron-clad case for her to give me her number and forget our silly agreement. But here she is, tempting more than Adam in the Garden of Eden.

I smile and lift my glass of whiskey to my lips. "That's entirely up to you, Kitten."

"Then tell me. What's this moment?" she asks, tracing the outline of my college team's mascot etched in traditional fashion.

"Bradshire University mascot wearing a championship ring around its neck. Go Mallards."

She runs her hands over the gargoyle beside it. "Moving up to the Renegades?"

I nod. "And winning a pennant my rookie year."

"And this one."

My heart hammers, and I'm hyper-aware of her nails as they trail up the inside of my thigh, incredibly close to where my balls are begging for her touch. "Cherry blossoms for my first trip out of the country to Japan. It's the trip that inspired me to want to see the world."

Her smug smile drives me wild, and I have no doubt she knows exactly what her touch is doing to me as she moves to the next piece.

"An umbrella to weather the storm that almost took my life when I was a kid, and the sun behind it as a reminder that it will always come out tomorrow."

"And this UFO?" She taps the tiny gray flying saucer.

"A memorial for a teammate taken too soon. He made believers out of all of us."

Her eyes lower to the floor reverently. "I'm sorry for your loss."

"Me, too."

She takes her time lingering on Red's memorial before gently moving my robe so it's covering only my cock and balls, exposing the rest of my leg to her. By the time her fingers reach my hip, teasing the sensitive flesh, I'm a mess of nerves. I know what tattoo is last. It's one I both love and hate because of what it meant and what it means now.

I swallow hard.

"And this?" It's the last one she touches.

My nostrils flare, and I swallow past the dread building in my throat. I don't want to ruin our night with Corinne's bullshit, but I won't lie to her either. "It was a crown for my queen, but now it's a reminder that I'm a king, even without her by my side."

"I like that," she muses, tracing the jewels inked into my skin before shifting her weight and standing.

Alarms sound in my head. She said she liked it, but the reminder of not only my ex but hers too, could've been too much of reality breaking through.

Fucking bastards. They don't get to ruin what could be.

Pshh.

Who am I kidding? There's no future here. This was always just one night. But I'm not ready to face that music yet. Right now, she's mine, and I'm not ready for it to end. Especially over two assholes who didn't deserve a single minute of our time.

I open my mouth to say as much, to tell her reality is overrated. Then she turns around, and I stop myself. Gone is the Willow who shares a piece of her mind, and in her place is a woman with a wicked grin and a mischievous stare. One that has me hanging on every rise of her perfect chest, desperate to know what she's going to say next.

CHAPTER ELEVEN
Willow

Even in a moment of panic, Bishop is altogether too damn handsome.

His frown gives away his thoughts. He thinks I'm about to leave again because of the mention of his ex. While I would love to tell you I am having a moment of clarity and prepared to do just that, that ship sailed the moment he asked to take care of me and proceeded to order everything on the menu. During the stories of his youth, I waved goodbye to logic and with the ink of his tattoos solidified my place in our realm of make-believe.

My lips twist into a playful grin meant to reassure him, but not quite divulge my plan just yet. I tap his thigh, a silent request for him to let me between his legs. He complies, his eyes never leaving mine. Which is fine by me, because I rather enjoy the weight of his stare—unnerving and empowering as it is.

"I read about your divorce," I start, running my fingertips over his thighs. "For what it's worth, I'm sorry for what happened, but not that she left you." I leave out the part where I thought she was a total cunt. I mean, who gives up a man like Bishop, let alone cheats on him? His ex was just like every other gold-digging social climber. I should know. I spent the last few months trying to get into their pocketbooks.

Bishop gives me a weak nod, and I wonder what's going through his mind. From the firm press of his lips and his jaw tight, I'd wager he's still trying to gauge where I'm headed with this conversation.

"I'm not sorry because if she hadn't, I wouldn't be here tonight and wouldn't have the opportunity to bow before a king."

I savor the way his mouth drops open, processing my words, and don't give him more than a second to think before shrugging my robe from my shoulders, leaving me bare for him.

"*Fuck*, Kitten," he groans.

A wry grin tips my lips, and I drop to the floor, my knees hitting the plush carpet. Starting at his knees, I drag the back of my fingernails up his thighs and under the hem of his robe, carefully avoiding the tent between his legs. He lets out a delightful hiss when I reach his hip bones and trace my way back down before repeating my path. Only this time, I tug his robes to the side and let his cock bounce free.

When my eyes zero in on his metal barbells and thick head, I'm almost ashamed of the way I lick my lips. Really, though, who could blame me? An ache builds between my legs, and I have no doubt I'm going to walk like a baby deer in the morning, but there are worse ways to start the new year.

My lips part on a gasp, and I lean down, running my tongue around the tip of his dick, teasing the slit before I pull back and look up at Bishop.

He's got one hand fisted at his mouth, his teeth digging into the flesh of his finger, while the other is white-knuckling the throw pillow beside him.

"Are you holding back for my sake, Mr. Lawson?" I tease.

"No, Kitten, I'm trying not to embarrass myself and come from just the sight of your tongue on my cock."

Leaning back on my heels, I smirk with a little shake of my head. "So you don't want me to continue."

I hope he doesn't tell me to stop. I plan to bring my A game and return the favor by ruining him for any other woman.

"I swear on every game I've played and have yet to play that if I don't get to see my cock between those pretty red lips and feel it hit the back of—"

That's all the encouragement I need. I don't let him finish his sentence before I grant his wish and wrap my lips around him, swallowing until he hits the back of my throat.

"Fuck," he growls as I pull back, letting my tongue rub the underside of his shaft slowly, swirling around each barbell. "God, your mouth is… it's…fuck."

My lips smile around him, and I take my time slowly working him from tip to root, only pausing when my nose nestles in the trimmed thatch of hair at the base of his shaft.

Bishop moans low and gravelly, and I shiver, making it my personal mission to hear it over and over.

"Fuuuuuuck, Kitten. That feels so fucking good. You take my cock like it was made for you."

His filthy comment has me humming around him and clenching my thighs together, living for his praise. I wasn't aware that was a turn-on for me, but all he has to do is whisper those salacious encouragements, and I'm a damn puddle.

My gaze flits up to his lust-filled eyes and I'm struck by the restraint he's still determined to hold on to.

That won't do. If I'm meant to fall apart, so is he.

Keeping my pace on his dick, I slide my hand up his thigh and over to his hand. Tangling my fingers with his, I bring his hand to the back of my head.

He hesitates and meets my gaze. I'm sure I'm a sight to see, choking on his dick, tears in my eyes and hair a mess, but still I will him to let go.

Fall with me. I dare you, I say with my eyes and moan around him.

It's only then he breaks.

Not needing further encouragement, Bishop entwines his fingers in my curls, digging them into my scalp. His hips, which up until now have remained stationary, begin to thrust upward, meeting my greedy mouth.

Gone is the cautious man who asks me if I'm okay, replaced once more by the caveman who feeds my darkest fantasies. He pistons his hips, his thrusts punishing as my jaw works to accommodate.

"You have no idea how fucking gorgeous you look. What I would give to see this every day," Bishop rasps.

The words slip from his mouth, and I'm not sure he realizes the weight of them or what it shakes loose inside me.

What if this could last? My core tightens at the thought, and I clench my thighs in an attempt to stop my arousal from dripping down my leg, but it's no use.

His balls tighten, and even though I am not usually one to swallow, I want everything Bishop has to offer.

I tighten my grip on his thighs and breathe in through my nose, mentally preparing myself for his release. Only it never comes. Instead of giving in like I know he wants to, Bishop tightens his hand in my hair and yanks me off of him.

"I wasn't finished," I growl, staring up at him from between his legs, confused by the wicked grin he's giving me. All I want is to taste him.

"As much as I'd love to shoot my come down your throat, I'd much rather see it dripping from your cunt."

On second thought, that does sound better.

I give him a short nod.

Bishop disentangles his hand from my hair before lacing his fingers behind his head.

He's a freaking masterpiece: tan skin against the dark sofa, tousled hair, a relaxed smile, and a studded cock standing straight up for good measure. I've never been one to picture specifics when touching myself, but this image will live rent-free in my mind for the rest of my life.

"Then ride me, Kitten."

My clit throbs as I pull myself from the floor and crawl into his lap. He hisses when I rock my hips, sliding his length through my arousal, before lifting myself to notch the tip of his cock at my entrance.

Anticipation settles low in my stomach as I lower myself inch by inch, feeling every single one of the rungs on his Jacob's ladder as it stretches the walls of my pussy.

Desperate and needy, my pubic bone hits his, and I let out a gasp, clenching down around him. Bishop's eyes widen, and his hands drop from behind his head, anchoring themselves in a bruising grip on the curve of my hips. "Fuck. If you want me to last, you can't do that."

"What if I don't want you to last?" I breathe, rolling my hips and dropping my forehead to his. I lift myself and slam back down his length, tightening around him once I'm fully seated once more. "What if I want you to come undone?"

His jaw tightens, and I can tell he's fighting for control. I shouldn't revel in it, but I do. I like him at my mercy just as much as I want to be at his.

"Tonight isn't about me," he grits out.

"I came first." I repeat the same motion with my hips, faster this time, and he digs his nails into the flesh at my waist. "Now I want you to come undone inside me."

"As appealing as that sounds, that's not how this works, Kitten," he growls. "You come first. Always. No matter how many times we do this, you will always come first."

Tonight, I've learned Bishop is a giver, but he's also as competitive as they come. Instead of giving in to the side of me that desires his praises, I rise to the occasion and issue a challenge of my own.

With both hands, I grasp the back of his neck and brush my thumb over the stubble of his jaw as I kiss him with everything I have. "Not if I can make you come first."

CHAPTER TWELVE
Bishop

I f it wasn't for the feel of her skin beneath my fingers or her pussy throbbing around my shaft, I might question if she was real.

This woman just challenged me, and the glint in her eye confirms she knows I won't back down. What she doesn't know is she doesn't stand a chance.

A plan forms in my mind, and I raise a confident brow. "Are you sure you want to play this game with me?"

Her breath hitches as she lifts herself to the tip of my dick. I expect her to continue her slow strokes, but then she surprises me, clamping hard around me and slamming herself down.

An involuntary moan tears from my throat as my dick fights for space in her tight cunt. "Fucking hell, Kitten."

She does it again, this time reaching up and plucking at her peaked nipples, and I take that as a yes.

She's more than willing to continue with her bet.

So be it.

Fuck, she's magic incarnate. Like a walk-off grand slam in the bottom of the ninth.

I fight for control, white-knuckling her hips while my breath spurts out in pants.

Our eyes stay locked on one another as she continues to tease me, and while I pride myself on my iron will, I'm already so close to coming. I just need to last a little longer. She needs to get herself close, and then I'll make her explode.

The smell of sex and the sounds of flesh meeting flesh spur us on, and I'm amazed by the woman on top of me. No longer the timid woman ashamed to ask for what she wants. Now she's taking it and making it her bitch. It only makes me want her more.

We start to build speed, and her hips begin to roll a little more each time she reaches the bottom of my shaft, forcing her clit against me.

"Bishop…this…fuck…"

My thoughts exactly, Kitten.

Her determined eyes narrow, and for a split second, I'm concerned by the knowing smile that curls her lips.

She thinks she's got me, but this time, I'm one step ahead of her.

I glance down at the discarded bag of toys beside us and bide my time.

Only a few more seconds.

That's when she throws a curveball. I should've known my little kitten would play dirty.

She clenches her pussy around me at the same time she reaches around and cups my balls, applying pressure to the sensitive spot between my sack and ass.

My body jerks upward as I suck in a hiss, followed by a guttural moan. She rides me with hard, languid thrusts while massaging that spot. "Holy fuck, Kitten."

I'm seconds away from losing it when Willow lets out a sound that's somewhere between a giggle and a whimper.

Fuck, this woman is incredible.

I force myself to think of anything to avoid coming. My grandmother. Dead puppies. Tomato sandwiches. But it's no use. All I feel is her.

Tingles shoot up my spine, and I know I've run out of time.

My hand darts from her hip and digs into the bag of toys, miraculously finding the one I'm looking for. It's a long purple vibrator in the shape of an eggplant of all things, something I'll give her shit about later. My thumb finds the switch with ease and skips to the third setting—the powerful constant buzz women love.

Her eyes widen, and I watch recognition dawn in her gaze. "No fai–"

The words die on her lips as I slip the shaking vegetable between us and crash it against her clit.

Willow's hands latch onto my forearms, and she digs her fingernails into my flesh.

"That's it, Kitten," I growl, a shit-eating grin on my face. "Come for me while I fill your pussy."

That's all the encouragement she needs.

Willow's back arches, and I marvel as she falls apart around me, screaming my name. It's enough to force me to follow her over the edge and shudder at my release into her.

My heart swells, but it only lasts a moment before crippling fear takes hold.

I don't want this to end.

Willow collapses on me, and even though I know we should clean up, I don't have it in me to move. I don't know how long we lay there, my cock still in her and her splayed on my chest, but I pray it never ends.

Her breathing grows steady, and when she finally lifts her head, her eyes are glassy with satisfaction.

A soft grin touches her lips. "Who won?"

"We both did, Kitten," I say, pushing a lock of hair away from her face.

"Good. I like winning with you."

I open my mouth to say more, but quickly close it. I want to make her promises and ask her to stay for more than just the night, but this moment is too perfect to ruin with thoughts of tomorrow.

Jackson is wrong. Willow's not like Corrine or any of the other women I've rushed into things with. They wanted me for what I offered, and Willow couldn't give two fucks because, unlike them, she's making her own name.

And I want to be along for the ride.

Right now, though, I just want it to be us for a little while longer.

The sheets are cold when I roll over.

I inhale the remnants of her citrus and mint shampoo, which I learned is specifically tailored for her curls. Curls I love tangling my fingers in. A smile finds its way to my lips as I roll over and untangle myself from the sheets, with the hope I might find Willow in the shower.

My smile falters a bit when the ensuite is empty and free of any sign of her. I continue my search, padding toward the main room. Silver domes and room service trays still litter most of the surfaces, but noticeably absent is the curvy little blonde I'm dying to have for breakfast.

"Willow?" I call out, hoping maybe she'd dropped an earring or something on the floor and would pop out from behind the bar or sofa.

Nothing.

My heart thunders in my chest as my eyes dart around the room, panic filling the spaces we'd forged a bond the night before.

A note written on the bar catches my eye, and I don't need to see the elegantly penned text on hotel letterhead to know who it's from.

Bishop,

Thank you for everything. Last night was the perfect way to ring in the new year. I wish you nothing but the best with everything with Corrine, but I think it's best if we part ways here. We'll always have New Year's.

Willow

She's gone.

She actually left.

My mind spins as I try to piece together what could have changed while we slept. I know it wasn't waking her up by feasting on her pussy. She made sure I knew how much she enjoyed that before we dozed off again.

And what the hell did she mean by wishing me the best with everything with Corrine?

I read the letter five more times, hoping it will magically make sense, but I'm left with more questions only Willow can answer.

Maybe she hasn't made it that far. What if she just left? She would have had to check out of her own room. Or maybe, if I'm lucky, she's still in the hotel.

A nagging feeling in my gut tells me our moment is over, but I refuse to believe it. I'm determined to get back what we started.

In seconds, I'm dressed and heading for the door when my phone rings. Without thinking, I answer it. Maybe it's her, even though we never exchanged numbers.

"Hello."

Instead of a sweet Kitten, I'm greeted by Jackson's growly timber. "Please tell me it's not true?"

"What?" I snap, instantly regretting answering. I don't have time for this.

"Oh shit, you haven't seen it."

The panic in Jackson's voice halts halfway to the elevator. "Seen what?"

"Check *The Foul Line*."

I pull the phone from my face and, ignoring the few texts from family and friends wishing me a happy New Year, pull up the website of the blogger who somehow manages to get all the dirt on our organization. It's where the city goes for their baseball news and where the big sports outlets get their dirt and fluff pieces.

Fuck.

I want to vomit when I read the headline at the top of the page.

CORRINE LAWSON PREGNANT WITH BISHOP LAWSON'S BABY AMID DIVORCE.

Everything clicks.

This is why she left. Willow must have seen this when she woke up and checked her phone.

If *The Foul Line* has it, then it's only a matter of time until the tabloids pick it up. If Corrine hasn't sold it to them already.

"Bishop?" Jackson's voice echoes from my speaker. "Bishop, what the hell is going on?"

I put the phone back to my ear and scrub my face with my free hand. "It's not true. You know I haven't slept with her in months. Seven to be exact. This is so fucked. Even if she did get pregnant the last time we slept together, she'd be so far along I would have been able to tell when we filed the divorce papers."

"Are you sure?"

"Yes, I'm sure," I bark. "I think I know when and where I came."

"Okay, I believe you." Jackson sighs, and I can picture him picking at his fingernails like he does when he's agitated. "How do you want to handle this?"

I want to go back to three hours ago when I was balls deep in Willow's cunt, without a thought of Corrine or the baby she's accusing me of fathering. I want to find a way to tell Willow this isn't me, and I'm not that kind of man. I want to beg her to understand and to remember the moments we shared between epic rounds of sex.

My stomach churns slowly, realizing that none of that is going to happen. It's not like I can call the owner of the Renegades and ask him for his daughter's number. It's not like I can prove Corrine is lying—at least not yet.

"Bishop?"

"I'll call my lawyer and then have Natalie set up a meeting with the Renegades PR team. I'm sure they'll want an explanation."

"I'll handle Nat. You just figure out how to get this under control."

"Thanks, Jackson."

"Anytime. How was your night?"

I hesitate, everything I want to tell my best friend on the tip of my tongue, but instead, I let out a weighted sigh. "It doesn't matter. New year, no pussy, remember?"

"It won't be that bad. And I didn't say no pussy." He scoffs.

He might as well have, because there's only one pussy I want at the moment, and when my year of relationship celibacy is over and my divorce is finalized, I plan to make it mine.

***

Thank you so much for reading MIDNIGHT RENEGADE!! I really hope you fell in love with Bishop and Willow as much as I did writing them. Need more of this incredible couple? Their story isn't over yet! There is a lot of heartbreak and healing in store for this duo, and I can't wait to take you along on their journey! You can CLICK HERE to preorder their full length book, RENEGADE RUIN.

***

I appreciate each and every one of you for taking this journey with me. Want to stay in the know about all my upcoming releases? Just sign up for my newsletter.

As an Indie Author, I would love your help spreading the word about MIDNIGHT RENEGADE. If you enjoyed the story, please consider leaving a review on Amazon, Goodreads, or even referring it to a friend.

Even a sentence or two makes a huge difference.

Thank you for taking this journey with me.

xoxo

Hayden

ALSO BY HAYDEN LOCKE

The Draft Series

MIDNIGHT RENEGADE (Prequel Novella)

RENEGADE RUINS (Bishop and Willow)

Love in Aspen

FINALLY HOME (Weston and Cami)

ACKNOWLEDGEMENTS

Whew! This was such a fun one to write.

When I set out to tell Bishop and Willow's story, I didn't plan to write this novella. But ask any writer and they will tell you sometimes the characters demand more of you. And these two definitely did. They wanted to show me what happened before the events of book one rock their world and so Midnight Renegade was born. And I'm so glad it was!

This story, hell, this pen name would have never come to life if it wasn't for a few very special individuals.

To my husband, my rock, my home: Thank you from the bottom of my heart. You allow me to dream big and make them into a reality. Even when you're gone for work you never stop cheering me on and helping me plot through any holes that pop up. Your fresh perspective and knowledge of the male orgasm is for ever and always appreciated!

To my daughters: Thank you for always reminding me everyone needs a break for cuddles. You guys are my world. #betheromance

To the book community:

Holy hell, I must say I am blown away by the kindness and support of authors, bookstagrammers and readers who have taken a chance on this new pen name and story. Every single time I am tagged in a gorgeous photo or video, I get a giddy smile on my face. You seriously make my day and inspire me to keep telling stories of boys in tight pants.

To my Book Bishes: Melissa, Christiana and Angel. You guys are my ride or die. This whole series is possible because you forced me to trust my gut and try something new. I live for our daily conversations and pictures of peens for science. This job can be a lonely one, but you guys make it not only bearable, but a damn pleasure.

To Silver: I am in complete awe of you and your ability to create incredible art from my ramblings. I am forever grateful that you took me on as a client and gave life to this story through art.

To Cass: You inspire me to believe in myself. I can never thank you enough for your friendship and guidance.

To Rachel: You are a gift from the editing gods. I am so glad we were able to work together. You made this book shine despite the fact that I am shit at commas. Your input is everything and I can't wait to work with you on the rest of the series!

And finally thank you to my readers.

Every. Single. One of you.

I wouldn't be here without you.

I am so grateful I get to do this job. Thank you for every sentence you read, every review you leave, every post you make. I see you. Thank you for taking a chance on me and my stories. You guys are magic.

xoxo

Hayden

ABOUT THE AUTHOR

Hayden is a California girl living in a North Carolina world…for now. After all, home is where the Army sends her husband next. When she isn't writing with music on way too loud, you can find her soccer momming it up, wrangling her two daughters into a game of hide and seek, or enjoying the finer things in life like supporting her favorites sports teams with an ice-cold beer in hand.

Stalk Hayden on her social media to find out what's coming up!